101 WAYS TO BUG YOUR TEACHER

101 WAYS TO BUG YOUR TEACHER

LEE WARDLAW

SCHOLASTIC INC.
New York Toronto London Auckland Sydney
Mexico City New Delhi Hong Kong Buenos Aires

ISBN 0-439-79106-5

12 11 10 9 8 7 6 5 4 3 2 1   5 6 7 8 9 10/0

Printed in the U.S.A.   40

First Scholastic printing, September 2005

Designed by Teresa Kietlinski
Text set in Caslon

For Linda Wiezorek (Miz Wiz)
with fond memories of my student teaching days
at Los Berros School, Lompoc, CA

My heartfelt thanks go out to:

. . . the teachers and students who helped create the 101 ways: Cara Leach's sixth graders, Foothill School, Santa Barbara, CA; Terry Ludlow's sixth graders, Pleasanton Middle School and Hart Middle School, Pleasanton, CA; Suzy Thompson's fourth graders, Pacheco School, San Luis Obispo, CA; Scott Williams's fifth graders, Loleta Elementary School, Loleta, CA; Dr. Judy Willis's fifth graders, Laguna Blanca School, Hope Ranch, CA

. . . the teachers who shared their chicken mummy experiences with me: Carla Detter, Media Specialist, Catawba Springs Elementary School, Denver, NC; Carla Leach; Scott Williams

. . . John M. Fox, MFT; Kristi Jensen McLoughlin, School Psychologist, Santa Barbara Junior High School; Suzie Thomas, WW

. . . my editor, Nancy Mercado, for her support and patience

. . . the best writer's group in the world, with love and admiration, ever and always: Ellen, Hope, Judy, Lisa, Marni, M1, M2, and Val xoxo

ONE

"HERE IT IS, gang," I announced, plunking a cloth-covered tray onto my school desk. "Behold and be dazzled! Our history project!" I whisked off the cloth, swirling it like a bullfighter's cape.

The four other members of my seventh-grade work group gazed with eager eyes.

Then their foreheads wrinkled.

And their mouths dropped open.

On the tray sat a mini-cooler, a box of salt, a roll of bandages, and . . .

"A chicken," Goldie said. "Our group project on ancient Egyptian culture is a *chicken*?"

"A four-and-one-quarter-pound chicken, to be exact," my best friend, Hiccup, announced, reading the label on the plastic wrapper. "With giblets."

"This eez not a history project," insisted Pierre. "It eez dinner! A little wine, a few mushrooms, simmer forty minutes, and voilà!"

"You've really laid an egg this time, Sneeze," Ace said with indifference.

"A chicken," Goldie repeated. She flipped a hunk of golden hair over one shoulder and peered around the classroom. Students sat clumped in busy groups of five, shoulders hunched, heads bent, voices a low buzz. "I don't get it. None of the other groups have a chicken."

"This isn't just any chicken," I defended. "At least, it won't be when we're finished with it."

"Are you gonna bring it back to life? Beware, it's Frankenchick! *Brawk!*" Hands tucked under her armpits, Goldie strutted and flapped, head pecking at invisible feed.

Pierre laughed so hard, his beret fell off.

Ace arched a dark eyebrow (which for anyone else would've been like pounding the desk in hysterics).

Several kids in the other groups chortled.

"Group Number Two." The smoldering voice scorched the room into silence.

I found Fierce, our world history teacher, regarding us with a look that ran goose blisters down my spine. She rose to her full four feet eleven inches and tugged at her buttoned navy blue blazer. The kids who'd chortled now cringed.

No one at Jefferson Middle School had ever seen Fierce (aka Ms. Pierce) get mad. No one wanted to. With that red hair flowing like lava and her ready-to-erupt tone, Fierce in miffed mode was dangerous enough.

"Group Two, is there a problem?" Fierce asked.

"No, no problem," I said. "Um, everything's under control."

"Then I suggest you sit and work quietly. Unless you'd prefer *the Death Roll.*"

Our class gave a collective shudder.

The Death Roll was Fierce's idea of "classroom management." If she caught you passing notes or whispering to your neighbor, you had to roll the dice kept in a box (marked with a skull and crossbones) on her desk. Then you matched the number with its mate on the Death Roll chart. There were twelve numbers in all, each describing different "disciplinary actions."

No simple detentions or demerits for Fierce. Her punishments were horrible things. Embarrassing things. I'd-rather-be-slathered-in-honey-and-staked-to-an-anthill things.

"No, no," I repeated. "We can work without the Death Roll, can't we, guys?"

Goldie, Pierre, and Hiccup bobbled their heads. I nudged Ace, who plucked an imaginary thread from his shirt and shrugged.

"Very well." With a last searing gaze, Fierce returned to grading papers.

The class gave a collective sigh. Hiccup set free a series of soft relief hics. He gets the hiccups whenever he's fidgety, frightened, frustrated, flustered, or flummoxed. (Frequently, he feels all five.)

"What *is* it with her?" whispered Goldie, thudding into her chair. "She's the meanest teacher ever. If only my mother were here. She could dig up some *information* about Fierce." An expression of sly glee spread over her face.

Goldie's mother was principal of our former elementary school. Although we'd been at Jefferson Middle School seven months, Goldie couldn't adjust to not having her mom around to meet her "educational needs."

Meaning juicy gossip.

3

"Contemplate revenge another time," I said. "And no, we're not going to bring the chicken back to life. We're going to prepare it for"–I paused for dramatic effect–"the *afterlife.*"

"You mean, like, hen heaven?" asked Goldie.

"Zee great chicken coop in zee sky?" Pierre put in.

Ace smirked.

"A word of warning," Hiccup said, eyeing the package. "Touch uncooked poultry, and you must wash your hands immediately with hot, soapy water. Otherwise, you risk contracting salmonella."

"Is that a fish disease?" Goldie asked.

Hiccup sighed. "Sal-mo-nel-la: a bacterial disease that causes–"

"Would you guys *please* let me finish?" I interrupted. "See, we'll mummify this chicken the way the Egyptians did with their dead pharaohs and queens, and–"

"I don't *believe* this," Goldie said, rolling her eyes. "Group One is molding gold-leaf burial masks. Group Three is building a papier-mâché replica of a sphinx. What are we doing? Putting Band-Aids on King Cluck!"

"That's a great name, Goldie," I said, jotting it in my notebook.

Pierre jerked his beret to one side. "This eez a disaster! We should have known better than to let you be in charge of zee project."

"Let me? *Let* me? Hey, you guys *begged* me to be chairman!"

"That's because you're supposed to be a genius," Goldie said.

4

"I'm not a genius," I insisted. "I'm an *inventor*."

"Then you should have *invented* a better idea for our project. Now we're doomed to flunk. Or worse, sink into obscurity–like all your inventions."

"I must protest," Hiccup said, half rising from his chair. His face flushed pink beneath its overdose of freckles. "Sneeze's inventions may be obscure now, but it is only a matter of time before they receive the recognition they deserve."

"Sit, Hic," I muttered. "It's okay. Really."

Ordinarily, I don't mind when Hiccup sticks up for my inventions. That's a best bud's job, right? But the last few weeks, I didn't feel I deserved it. The last few weeks, a secret had been gnawing deep inside me like a fanged rat. A secret so sharp, I couldn't even share it with my best friend.

"No, it is *not* okay," Hiccup insisted, his voice rising with near patriotism. "I cannot let you, or your project"– he placed a protective hand on the chicken–"be insulted. Let the rest of our group cry–"

"Fowl!" Goldie put in.

"–failure," Hiccup said. "Let the group snicker and–"

"Cackle!" said Pierre.

"–scoff," Hic persisted. "You do not need them, Sneeze. You can stand alone on your own two–"

"Drumsticks!" Goldie cried.

Pierre fell off his chair, chortling.

"Group Number Two." Fierce's words branded the air.

"Um, yes?" My voice quavered.

"Death Roll."

"No, no! Wait! We didn't mean to—"

"Death Roll. Now."

Goldie groaned. Hiccup moaned.

"We are," Pierre mumbled, "how you say . . . toast."

Fierce crooked a finger at Ace. "You first."

Ace sauntered toward her desk. The class sat in solemn silence as if watching a funeral procession. One kid started to hum the music from *Jaws,* but squeaked off in mid *da-dum-da-dum* when Fierce caught him with a flame-thrower glance.

Ace picked up the dice. Then, with a bored yawn, he turned his hand over and . . . bombs away!

The dice fell to the desk with a single *clack.*

"Seven," Fierce said.

The class gasped. Pierre gave a low whistle.

Ace is not only the coolest guy I know, he's also the luckiest.

Number seven is: *Probation. No punishment.*

Ace shrugged as if to say *of course,* and meandered back to his desk.

Fierce pointed at Hiccup. "Next!"

Hiccup gulped, but marched toward the dice. He jiggled them in his palm, then spilled them across the desk.

"Four," Fierce said.

I slumped in my chair. Number four is: *Sing three verses of "Old MacDonald Had a Farm."*

Hic stared at us like we were snorting rhinoceroses, ready to stampede.

"We're waiting," Fierce said, arms folded with impatience.

6

Hiccup blinked. Cleared his throat. Then warbled off-key:

"Old *hic!*–Donald had a farm. E-*hic!*-E-*hic!*-O! And on *hic-hic!* he had some *hics!* E-*hic!*-E-*hic!*-O!"

A wave of laughter rippled through the room, even though Fierce's eyes seemed to snap and crackle like green flame. Hiccup's face blanched fish-belly white, his freckles popping out in 3-D. His lower lip trembled. Still, he kept singing.

And hicking.

"Here a *hic!* There a *hic!* Everywhere a *hic-hic!*"

The kids laughed harder.

Hiccup's face turned chalky.

Fierce's eyes blazed greener.

I couldn't let it go on. I *wouldn't.*

I leaped from my chair. *"Ms. Pierce–!"*

The end-of-class bell rang.

Fierce's hand clapped onto Hiccup's shoulder. "Group Two will stay," she commanded. "The rest of you are dismissed."

Students snatched papers and books, and pushed past us, cramming through the door before Fierce could change her mind.

"Uh, excuse, Miz Pierce," Pierre said, twisting his beret in his hands. "I cannot be late for home economics class. Today I bake zee croissants."

"And I've got a deadline for the newspaper," Goldie broke in. "My gossip column, you know."

I shuffled from one foot to the other. "Um, and I have to go to the bathroom." (Preferably in Ohio.)

7

Ace gave a luxurious cat-stretch, settling deeper into his chair. He looked as if he didn't have to be anywhere important. Ever.

"You will stay." Fierce's green eyes flared hotter.

"Um, sure, if you put it that way," I answered.

The five of us took a deep breath. Then we shuffled forward to face the crematorium that was Ms. Pierce.

TWO

"SIT," FIERCE COMMANDED.

We sat.

Or, rather, we bumped backward into the nearest seats, not daring to take our eyes off her. (All except Ace, who started buffing his fingernails.)

She hitched up onto her favorite stool, the one we'd nicknamed The Tower. That's because it's so tall, even a shrimp like Fierce towers over everyone when sitting on it.

Fierce straightened her already-straightened jacket, then fixed each one of us with a long, blazing gaze. Hic's hiccups immediately revved into overdrive. He struggled to swallow them, which only produced the same *huck-huck* sound his cat makes when hawking up a fur ball.

"Is that dinner?" Fierce asked me. "Or just a friend?"

I looked down to find I still held King Cluck.

"Oh, um, *this*?" I gave a nervous laugh. "This is our Egyptian project."

"No, it's not!" Goldie blurted.

"Yes, it is," I shot back.

"No, it eez *not*," Pierre broke in.

"*HUCK-HUCK. HUCK HUCK,*" said Hic.

Fierce closed her eyes for a long moment. The room temperature dropped ten degrees, like when a stray cloud passes over the desert sun.

"Mr. Denardo, go get a drink from the hall fountain," she instructed.

Hiccup bolted. He must've been beyond desperate to get out of there, because he never drinks anything but bottled water. Fluoride phobia, you know. Don't ask.

"As for the rest of you," Fierce continued, her voice simmering, "you will stop stalling and start working *together* on this project. The History Faire is only three weeks away, and you *will* be ready. Your project counts as fifty percent of your final grade. That should be of particular interest to you, Mr. Wyatt, since you currently have a solid F average in this class, if you get my drift."

Drift? Ha. More like being swept over Niagara Falls.

I scrubbed at my nose. Just the hint of spending another year with Ms. Pierce made it tickle.

And tingle.

And itch.

"*Ahhhh*-CHOOEY!" I let loose with a trademark Niagara Falls of my own.

"I'll take that as a yes," Fierce said as I mopped my nose. "You will have a project chosen, and your individual research notebooks begun, by tomorrow. No exceptions. Are there any questions?"

There weren't.

"I'll see you then." Fierce waved us away like we were pesky flies.

We leaped up before she had a chance to swat us, shoveling books and papers into our packs. I dumped King Cluck into the cooler, then raced to follow Goldie and Pierre out the door. Ace sauntered behind, hands in his pockets. He's too cool to carry anything except a pencil stub, which he keeps tucked behind one ear.

We pushed through the stream of students flowing noisily toward their next class, and found Hiccup across the hall. He was sipping and grimacing at the tepid water that dribbled from the drinking fountain.

"What *hic!* transpired in *there*?" he asked.

Was that a shiver I heard in his voice?

"We are up the Nile without a paddle," Goldie said.

"More like without zee boat," Pierre grumped with a snooty glance toward Fierce's door. "What eez her problem? She always treats us like we are bank robbers or Jack zee Ripper. In Paris, the women are as sweet as they are young and pretty!"

"Oh, like you've been to Paris," Goldie said. "You live in Ca-li-for-ni-a, Pierre. Get over it."

Pierre ignored her. "Fierce want us to have zee Egyptian project begun by tomorrow," he explained to Hic. "Which eez impossible now that we know zee truth." He glared at me.

"What truth?" I asked.

"That you're flunking history!" Goldie said with an angry toss of her mane.

"Oh, that." The F was bad, but the least of my worries.

"If my mother was principal of Jefferson," Goldie went on, "I would've known about that F even before *you* did.

11

And I never would've let you talk us into putting you in charge of our project."

"You–*let*–?" I sputtered, my face aflame.

"Excuse *hic!* me," Hiccup broke in. "This incessant bickering is causing an attack of gastroesophageal reflux."

"What's that?" Goldie's question held a hint of horror–and hope of horror.

"Heartburn," Ace said with a yawn from where he'd been lounging against a row of lockers.

The one-minute-warning bell rang.

"You're right, Hic," I said. "Fighting isn't getting us anywhere, except late for class. Let's meet at my house tonight, and we'll make a final decision about our project. Is seven o'clock okay?"

"Under one condition," Pierre said. "You will fix my electric beaters, yes? Zee high speed eez broken. I cannot get zee egg whites to make stiff peaks."

"Sure, okay, fine," I said, hearing a tiredness in my tone. Last week it had been Goldie's hair dryer. The week before, two cell phones and four beepers belonging to kids in my science and math classes. And then, my PE teacher hit me up to fix his *whistle*.

Funny, but last year at this time, I wanted nothing more than for everyone to know I was a whiz with a wrench.

Well, okay, what I *really* wanted was to be a rich, famous, and respected inventor. What I really wanted was to be *liked*.

For six years no one except Hiccup had ever wanted to be my friend. No one, except Hiccup, ever invited me to the movies or to play soccer or to go out for pizza. Who could blame them? I was just that nerdy kid with the terminal allergies who wore a tool kit attached to his belt, sneezed a bazillion times a day, and always had a wet nose like some big dumb dog.

My chance at fame, fortune, and friendship finally came when I invented the Nice Alarm, an alarm clock that wakes you *nicely* by tapping you on the shoulder. A novelty company was interested in buying the idea, and asked me to meet with the boss at the annual Invention Convention® in San Francisco.

Wow. My dream come true!

The problem? I live in Lemon County, more than 500 miles away. My parents couldn't afford to take me to San Francisco, so I devised a brilliant plan. During my summer creative writing class, I wrote a book called *101 Ways to Bug Your Parents* and sold copies in the boys' restroom to raise money for the trip.

I became a sudden superstar. *Everyone* loved the book.

Well, okay, everyone *except* the parents, the teachers, the school board . . .

Anyway, soon after, my celebrity status plunged from hero to handyman. Now people saw me only as a genius Mr. Fix-It, expecting me to be ready, willing, and able to tinker with everything from school projects to washing machines.

To make matters worse, I didn't earn enough money to attend the convention. I'd vowed to get there this summer, though. No. Matter. What.   .

"Ace, will you be joining us at Sneeze's tonight?" Goldie's question interrupted my thoughts.

"Maybe I will," Ace replied with a yawn, "and maybe I

won't." He ambled down the hall in the opposite direction of his next class.

The final bell rang.

"We're late!" Goldie squealed, flinging a lank of hair and her pack over one shoulder. "Hey—isn't that the Queen of the Clubs?"

July Smith sailed out of the Student Activities office, her chocolate-colored cape rippling in her wake.

"I've heard," Goldie said in breathless awe, "that she's joined forty-nine clubs in the two years she's been here. *Forty-nine!* I'll bet she just signed up for the big five-oh. What a scoop for my column!" She groped in her pack for her *Goldie's Gossip* notebook and tape recorder, and streaked down the hall. "Hey, July—wait up!"

Hic and I had math together next. "Let's go, buddy," I said.

"I be—*hic!*—lieve," he replied, "that I shall lie down in Tony's office for the interim."

Tony Sandoval is the school nurse. Everyone else at Jefferson has to call him Mr. Sandoval. But since Hiccup and I drop by to see him at least once a day—me, to take my allergy medicine; Hiccup, because of various maladies ("small pox," aka his first zit; "scurvy," the morning he forgot to drink his orange juice . . .)—Tony lets us call him by his first name.

I peered into Hic's face. "Are you okay?" Silly question since, according to Hiccup, he is never okay. But he seemed less okay than usual.

"This prolonged spasmodic ep—*hic!*—sode," he

answered, "combined with the questionable sanitation of the alleged drinking water, has left me with vertigo."

I didn't know what vertigo was, and I wasn't about to ask. Hiccup would've spent eight days telling me. With flow charts and diagrams.

"Okay, I'll let Miss Aguilar know where you are," I said. "See you on the bus. Same row, same seat, as always."

He flipped a thumbs-up and hicked his way down the hall.

"See you tonight, Pierre," I added.

"Wait." Pierre grabbed my shirt and leaned so close, my forehead almost touched his beret. "As a chef, I give a little advice for zee meeting, yes? If you know what is good for you, you will take zee chicken and . . . stuff it!"

THREE

"YOU COMIN', HON?" The school bus driver tossed her words at me over the clatter-wauling of the engine.

Worried, I scanned the lawn area and entrance to the school. Only a few kids left, hanging out by the main doors.

Where was Hiccup? He should've been here by now. He always beats me to the bus . . .

"I got a schedule to keep, you know," the driver warned. The other buses were pulling away in a hail of backfire. "In or out, hon." She revved the engine. Exhaust spewed from the tailpipe, swirling leaves and dust in a tornado of fumes.

I sneezed. "Fibe bore binutes," I begged.

"What?"

I blew my nose. "Five more minutes. You owe me one, remember?"

She drummed her fingers on the steering wheel, not daring to look at me. She hated reminders of the day she'd accidentally hit the Close Door button too soon, squishing Goldie like an accordion and jamming the auto-open mechanism. If it hadn't been for my quick thinking and trusty tool kit, the driver would've read about herself in Goldie's next headline: POPULAR GOSSIP COLUMNIST SQUEEZED LIKE TOOTHPASTE IN BUS ACCIDENT; DRIVER WITH ITCHY TRIGGER-FINGER BLAMED.

The driver sighed. "*Two* minutes," she said.

"Thanks!" I dumped King Cluck's cooler-tomb at the base of the flagpole, then sprinted into school.

No sign of Hiccup in his last class. Ditto for the boys' restroom.

Wait—could he still be with Tony?

I about-faced toward the nurse's office.

"I was expectin' you," Tony said in his western drawl when I skidded, out of breath, through the door.

Hiccup, covered by a wool army blanket, lay on his favorite cot by the window. He struggled to say hi, but it came out more like *hike*.

Tony shook his head. "Worst case of hiccups I've seen him get yet. I tried every cure I know: drinkin' sugar water, eatin' crushed ice, slight pressure on the eyeballs. None of it worked, so I called his folks. I think a little R and R at home is just the ticket."

Ha. Rest and relaxation was the *last* thing Hiccup would get at the Denardo house. His family consists of six boys, eight dogs (named after Santa's reindeer), one cat, and an unimaginable number of fleas. Which probably explains why Hiccup spends so much time at *my* house.

Hiccup raised himself on one elbow. "But, Tony, now I will be unable to assist Sneeze at his place of employ-ment! I am his right-hand *hic!* man."

"So I'll be a lefty today," I said. "It's only one afternoon. You should rest. Besides, didn't you want to finish this month's episode of MM?"

Hiccup writes and draws a comic book about a superhero named Medicine Man. *I vow not to rest until I wipe out the disease of injustice!* is MM's motto as, green cape snapping in the breeze, he whacks thugs with a stethoscope and prescribes aspirin, bed rest, and plenty of liquids for the victims.

"Oh, yes!" Hic said, his face brightening. "In this issue, MM eradicates the common cold *and* the common criminal, all in one *hic!* morning!" He threw off the blanket and zipped into the bathroom. I heard water splashing in the sink.

Tony jerked up the pants legs of his green scrubs, revealing a scuffed pair of cowboy boots, and sat on the edge of his desk. "Don't fret," he said. "Hiccup will be fit as a fiddle tomorrow, riding shotgun with you at work, on the bus–"

"The *bus*! I gotta go, man. See you tonight, Hic!" I hollered through the bathroom door. "Hope you feel better by then. Bye, Tony!"

I jammed out of his office. Thundered along the hall. Leaped down the front steps three at a time.

Too late. My bus was gone . . . and, a quick glance toward the flagpole revealed, so was King Cluck.

"Grave robbers!" I yelled, but there was no one left to hear.

Rats. Now I'd have to dip into my Invention Convention® fund to replace the cooler *and* the hen.

18

Maybe I could convince the history group to chip in. Of course, first I had to convince them that a mummified chicken was a great idea. Judging from their reactions– and Pierre's threat–that would take some work.

Work. Oh, man. I was going to be late for work! Facing my boss when she got mad was almost as bad as facing Fierce.

I grabbed my pack and set off on the long jog to Gadabout Golf.

***

"You're *late*," a voice announced in a mixture of anger and wonder. "You're *never* late." Hayley Barker. Age thirteen. Short bobbed hair the color of rice. Dangly golf ball earrings. Blue eyes cold as ice cream eaten right out of the deep freeze. My number two best friend and the boss at Gadabout Golf.

Hayley's dad owns the funky miniature golf course where I do maintenance work on mechanical stuff, like the burbling Volcano (Hole #7) and the drawbridge on King Arthur's Castle (Hole #15). But Hayley's practically been running the place since her mom died in a car crash three years ago.

And she's right. I'm *never* late. In fact, I'm always early. And I love to work overtime. Gadabout Golf is my *sanctuary.*

Okay, so with its lime green AstroTurf "grass," the thirty-year-old recording of burping moat-frogs, and the plastic palm trees that smell like Scotch tape, it's not exactly the Garden of Eden. But it's where my brain hums like a cordless drill . . . where every screw I twist tightens straight and true . . . where my ideas mesh and move like a well-oiled wheel.

And where that little rat of a secret stays deep in its hole.

"Sorry I'm late, boss," I said, meaning it. I hung my set of Gadabout keys—a Christmas gift from Hayley—on their special hook in the office. Then I reached under the front counter for my Gadabout T-shirt and name tag. "I missed the bus," I added.

Hayley put down the putter she'd been polishing. Leaning on one elbow, she zapped me her famous SOS: Squint of Suspicion. A look that forced even the toughest of toughs to obediently return clubs and balls after a game. A look that never failed to make *me* want to confess to crimes I hadn't committed.

"Honest. I missed the bus," I repeated. "I had to run the whole way."

Hayley snorted, but went back to polishing the putter. "I'll have to dock you forty-five minutes of pay," she said.

"Make it an hour and forty-five," I confessed. "I gotta leave early. My Egyptian group's meeting at my house tonight, and we've a ton of work to do. Fierce is in fire-breathing mode."

Hayley snorted again. "She's a teacher, not a dragon."

"So *you* say, but *you* don't have her for world history. *You* didn't see Hiccup's face when she humiliated him." I filled her in on our friend's "recital."

Her eyes widened, and she let out a gentle sigh. "Oh, poor Hic!" She turned to take money from three boys who had stepped up to the counter. "Hey, are you chewing gum?" Her eyes flashed the SOS. "Well, spit it in the trash. No gum chewing at Gadabout. 'Cuz I'm the one who has to scrape it up, that's why."

Not true. Last month, the water filter in King Arthur's moat conked out. Took me a whole afternoon to clean up the problem: a collection of ABC gum wads the size of a pot roast clogging the works.

"Daddy's at the barber shop," Hayley said. "I don't know why. I *like* his hair long and shaggy, but–" She stopped as if about to tell me something else, then changed her mind. "Anyway, he wants you to work on Big Ben. The clock is 'boinging' instead of 'bonging.'"

"I'll get right on it," I said, snatching the keys off the hook.

As I headed for Hole #9, I heard Mr. Barker's car crunch across the gravel parking lot, sputtering to a stop. "Hayley!" he called. "Where are you, Peach?"

Hayley was suddenly beside me, arm clutching my elbow, ushering me along so fast, I almost tripped.

"Hey–!"

"Let me show you where to go," she said, picking up the pace.

"I've worked here for almost a year. I think I know where Big Ben is." We were, in fact, standing in its shadow.

"I mean, let me show you what the problem is."

"But your dad is calling you."

"Hayley, honey!" Right on cue.

"I didn't hear anything," Hayley insisted. "Come *on*."

She clutched me harder and we chugged to the back of the course, where she darted behind Ben.

"You can fix the problem from in there," she said in a hoarse whisper, pointing at a small trapdoor at the base of the clock.

"I know. First I want to hear what he sounds like."

"No! *Don't.*"

"Hayley, my skills are like a doctor's," I said with professional authority. "I have to listen to Ben's 'chest' before I can make a diagnosis." Hiccup would've loved that analogy. I chuckled, and dropped a stray golf ball through the hole-in-one slot.

BOY-YOY-YOING. BOY-YOY-YOING. BOY-YOY-YOING.

"Ah-ha!" said Hayley's dad with a grin, making his way toward me. "Here's someone I recognize."

"Thanks a lot!" Hayley spat the whispered words, and crammed herself into the thorny hedge behind me.

What was going on?

"Hi, Mr. Barker," I said. "I was just about to fix ol' Ben here."

"Were you now? That's fine, just fine." He jingled the coins in his pocket, a happy jig of a sound that matched the dancing hula girls on his Hawaiian shirt. His blond hair, the curls cropped short and slicked back, looked dark with some kind of goo. He smelled like oranges and eucalyptus.

"Have you seen Hayley?" he asked.

"Ouch," she replied. "Oh, *golf tees.*" It was the closest to a cuss word I'd ever heard her use.

"I've been looking all over for you," Mr. Barker said, peering into the hedge.

"Oh! Hi, Daddy. I didn't know you were back." She shot me a glance that dared me to contradict her.

She struggled to move, but the thorns had her snagged. "I was just, um, looking for lost balls and got–*ouch*–stuck."

"We'll have you out in a jiffy," Mr. Barker reassured, "won't we, Sneeze?"

Together we unhooked the thorns caught in her sweater and one earring.

"Daddy," Hayley said, wrinkling her nose, "you . . . *smell*."

"I love you too," Mr. Barker chuckled. "It's called a pomade. The barber said it would keep my new hairstyle in place. Don't you like it?"

"Oh, um, sure," she answered, with barely a glance. "It looks very . . . wet. I've got to get back to the counter now. There could be hoodlums up there, stealing cash from our register."

"Hold on," her dad said, reaching for her hand. "You never gave me an answer about tonight. Daisy and I would really like you to join us."

A rosy spot bloomed on each of Hayley's cheeks. "Daddy, I don't–"

"Just burgers and a movie. I think it's about time you met her. What do you say, Peach?"

Hayley got a sad, pinched expression at the mention of her pet name. "Um, not tonight. I–I'm going over to Sneeze's. We're having an important meeting for our class Egyptian project."

"But," I began, "you're not–"

She cleared her throat as sharply as a swift kick in the ankles. I winced, took the hint, and shut my mouth.

"Well, okay." Mr. Barker jingled the coins in his pocket

again, but their dance sounded forced, tired. "Okay," he repeated. "Schoolwork comes first, right? Maybe next weekend. Get lots done tonight. I'll fetch you after I take Daisy home." He kissed Hayley on the forehead and darted away, his flip-flops slap-slapping as he hurried back up the path.

"I think his hair looks silly," Hayley said in a quiet voice. "Don't you think it looks silly? He's a *dad,* not a rock star."

"What's going on?" I asked. "Why are you coming to my house tonight when you're not even in Fierce's class? And who is Daisy?"

Hayley bit her lip and looked away, arms crossed against her chest.

I unlocked Ben's trapdoor with one of my keys. With a click, I shone a flashlight into the clock's innards, breathing in the oily, metallic aroma of mechanisms, pulleys, and gears. Ah. Home, sweet home.

"Daisy is Daddy's girlfriend," Hayley announced.

"His *what*?!" I bonked my head backing out of Ben. "How long has this been going on?"

She shrugged. "I don't know. I don't care. All I know is, she's not taking Mom's place. She's *not.*"

"Why didn't you tell me before?" I asked.

Hayley sat down on London Bridge, dangling her legs over the edge. "I didn't want it to be true. If I said it aloud, if I told you, that would make it real, wouldn't it?"

I nodded—then almost told her. Almost told her my secret. The sharp little secret that, like hers, had been nesting and gnawing inside me for weeks. But I couldn't say the words, because she was right. If I said them aloud, they'd be true, they'd be real. I couldn't bear them to be real, those four little words:

I had inventor's block.

FOUR

"I'M HOME!" I called, slamming the front door.

I switched on Coat Away, the automatic coat remover I'd invented last Thanksgiving. With a click and a whir, the metallic fingers reached out to ease the Windbreaker off my shoulders. I held my breath. Maybe *this* time . . .

No such luck. The fingers squeaked and slipped, streaking ten black, oily lines down my back. Rats. Another jacket that looked like a zebra. At this rate, I'd soon have a whole herd.

"In here," a groggy voice called from the living room.

I yanked off the Windbreaker, stuffing it into my pack so Mom wouldn't see. I found her lying on the couch, eyes closed, stockinged feet propped on a pillow. She still wore her white lab coat (Mom's a microbiologist), a wet washcloth draped across her forehead.

My insides gave a squeeze. "Are you okay?"

Despite the fact that Mom spends almost every day peering through her microscope at bugs with ominous-sounding names, she's *never* sick.

She opened her eyes and gave a pale smile. "I'm queasy. There's a twenty-four-hour flu going around the lab."

"Do I need to cook dinner?" I offered, although I knew

she'd say no. She hadn't let me fix anything more difficult than a glass of milk since I rigged up an Instant Guacamole Maker in our refrigerator's water dispenser. For three months we got avocado-flavored ice cubes.

"*NO!*" Mom insisted. "I mean, no, thank you, honey. Your dad's cooking."

"I thought I smelled ketchup." Dad's two favorite "spices" are ketchup and salsa. Which is fine if we're having French fries or tacos, but not spaghetti or mashed potatoes.

Mom groaned. "Don't even whisper the word ketchup. It makes me woozy." She plunked the washcloth over her entire face. "You had three messages on the answering machine," she muffled. "A broken lawn mower, a toaster stuck on 'self-immolation,' and something about Mrs. Rose's dog."

"What, no washing machines?" I grumbled.

"Oh, and Hiccup's mom called about her washing machine."

I sighed and headed for the staircase. The washer was probably eating Hic's medicated socks again. "I'll call everyone back later. My history group's coming at seven to work on our project. That okay?"

She flapped a weak hand, which I took to mean yes.

Upstairs, the Nice Alarm greeted me from the desk with a chipper *tick-tick, tick-tick*. My chest swelled with a balloon of pride. The alarm was my finest achievement. Seeing it never failed to make me stand a little straighter . . . even though I feared it might end up my *only* achievement.

Don't think about that. DON'T.

I glanced around. Posters of Bill Gates, Ben Franklin, and Galileo did a good job of covering the pistachio and strawberry splotches that had stained my walls ever since the electronic ice cream cone I'd invented (for kids too lazy to lick) went berserk. But the rest of the room needed a quick fix, especially if I didn't want Goldie writing about my underwear in her next gossip column.

I shoved wads of dirty clothes and tissues into my bed, covering them with the flannel comforter. Containers of nuts, bolts, screws, springs, and tools went into the closet. I locked my invention journals (where I'd kept detailed records of all my creations since the age of six) in the bottom drawer of my desk.

"Hi, guys," I said. "Dinnertime." The aquarium bubbled with exuberance. I sprinkled food flakes into the water and watched as Edison, Bell, and the Wright Brothers slurped away, their tails squiggling like a dog's when asked if he wants to go for a walk.

Only one fish, a cobalt blue neon tetra, ignored the meal, his mouth blowing pretend smoke rings.

"Who," I said, "are . . . *you?*"

I didn't own a neon tetra.

A gift, maybe?

Not my birthday.

A replacement fish?

But I hadn't told Mom or Dad about Hyman L. Lipman (named after the inventor of the first eraser-tipped pencil) passing away. I'd given him a private "burial at sea" in the toilet a few weeks ago.

That could mean only one thing.

My stomach grew cold, like I'd chugalugged a pitcher of icy lemonade.

"Daaaa-AAAAD!" I scooped the tetra into an empty pencil mug and marched down to the kitchen.

I found Dad holding a bouquet of silverware. I tapped him on the shoulder and demanded: "What. Is. This."

With a patient smile, he patted my arm. "It's a pencil holder, Steve."

"No," I said, exasperated. I shook the holder in his face, causing the tetra to almost splash out in a baby tidal wave. *"This."*

Dad peered into the mug, his forehead as rumpled as his sweater. "I don't have my glasses," he said, "but it appears to be a fish. And a few soggy pencil shavings."

"It's a bribe, isn't it?"

"We-ell . . ." Dad waved the bouquet in a vague circle. "I don't much care for that word. I prefer to think of it more as . . . incentive."

The icy-lemonade feeling in my stomach spilled into my veins.

Whenever Dad is about to drop an Atom Bomb of Disappointment on my life, he brings me a tropical fish (the only kind of pet that doesn't make me sneeze). The last detonation had been nine months ago, when he and Mom announced we couldn't afford to go to San Francisco and the Invention Convention®. They tried to defuse their bomb with a new fish, but I felt so betrayed that I dubbed him Benedict Arnold and set out on a summer-long Parental Bugging Marathon (which is how I got the idea for my book). Edison and the gang must've felt betrayed too, because their fishy tribunal sentenced Traitor Ben to a watery execution: One morning, exactly at dawn, they *ate* him.

I thudded into a chair. "Dad, you and Mom promised you would never spring important stuff on me again. We're supposed to talk to each other first, remember?"

Last year, after I got sent to the principal's office for selling *101 Ways to Bug Your Parents* in the boys' restroom, Mom, Dad, and I made a deal: I'd start talking to them–not bugging, but really *talking*–and they promised to start listening and including me in major decisions.

"What happened to us discussing stuff *together?*" I asked.

"We planned to have a family chat after dinner," Mom said from where she now stood dizzily in the doorway. She made a slow, careful path across the kitchen and eased herself into the chair next to mine. "But since your group will be here soon, we should probably talk now."

"Dinner is served!" Dad said. With a flourish he set plates in front of us.

The steaming conglomeration looked familiar. I poked at it with my fork. "What *is* this?"

"Meatloaf fajitas!" he announced, looking pleased with himself. In the middle of the table he plunked bottles of both salsa *and* ketchup. Dad had invented his ideal meal.

Mom gulped and pushed her plate aside. "I–I think I'll just have some tea." She picked up the pencil mug and, before I could stop her, raised it to her lips. She and the tetra eyed each other for a long moment. Then Mom's face changed from bleached-bone white to a greasy green. "Excuse me," she whispered, and bolted into the bathroom.

"Are you all right, Barb?" Dad called after her.

"No."

"She'll be all right," Dad reassured me. "Dig in!"

I crossed my arms. "Not till you tell me what's going on."

Dad spooned chunks of meatloaf and stir-fried veggies into a tortilla, then splunked globs of ketchup and salsa on top. "Don't panic. This is a good thing, honest," he began, taking a large, squelchy bite.

I didn't know if he meant the dinner or the topic of our family "discussion." I hoped both, but I had my doubts.

Dad chewed blissfully for a moment, then said: "Your mom and I have had several meetings with the principal and your teachers at Jefferson. We all agree—well, almost all—that your classes are way too easy for you."

So what else was new? I'd known that since my first hour in day care, when the other kids used Lincoln Logs to build a tiny, roofless cabin and I built a nuclear power plant.

"You're a bright young man," Dad was saying. "Too bright for what this middle school can offer. Your mind needs to be challenged! Your curiosity aroused, not numbed into boredom."

"Whooooa," I said, taking a sip of milk and practicing Hayley's SOS. "You're not signing me up for another summer school writing class, are you?"

Dad shook his head. "Better. We've arranged for you to"—he paused, as if waiting for a drumroll—"skip eighth grade and start in the fall at Patrick Henry High!"

I choked on my milk till some shot out my nose.

"High school?!" My voice squeaked at last. "But I'm only twelve!"

"You'll be thirteen this fall," Dad replied. "And your mental abilities are years older than that. Right, Barb?"

From the bathroom, Mom made a sound like an old steer dying on the prairie.

"You'll get to take advanced college-prep classes," Dad went on, "and use their new computer and science labs. The high school even has a beginning engineering program and a state-of-the-art workshop. This is a tremendous opportunity for you and your inventions. We're so proud of you, right, Barb?"

"Right," Mom said, shuffling back into the kitchen. She gave a wan smile, but now she *looked* like an old steer dying on the prairie—with the vultures circling.

"So what do you think?" Dad asked.

What could I say? A year ago, I would've jumped at the chance. Engineering classes. A real workshop. Wow. But now . . .

"Steve . . . ?" Mom prompted.

How could I tell them my life as an inventor might be over? Sure, I'd been able to put the finishing touches on the gizmos and gadgets I'd invented before Christmas. But since then, I hadn't had one single new idea. Nothing. Nada. Nix. Zippo. Zero. Zilch. The Big Goose Egg.

"I can't believe you made all these plans without asking me first," I said, anger swelling my voice. I stabbed at the taco stuff and shoved it into a tortilla, wrapping it tight till I had a meatloaf mummy.

"We didn't want to get your hopes up," Mom explained.

"We weren't sure we could convince everyone that you're ready," Dad added. "We had to meet with the principals from both schools, your guidance counselor, and–"

"What about my friends?" I demanded. "Hiccup and Hayley. I'll have to leave them behind!" My stomach churned at the thought. "I've never fit in at school with anyone except them!"

Mom filled the kettle for tea and set it to boil. "That's one of our concerns. Also, there's a teacher at Jefferson who fears you may not be–how did she put it, David?– 'socially mature enough' to handle high school."

Dad nodded. "You never get involved in activities or clubs. You don't like to make new friends or try new things. That will make it tougher to adjust to high school, where everyone will be so much older than you."

"I don't have time to make new friends or join a bunch of clubs," I said. "I'm too busy with my inventions and my job at Gadabout. I still want to take the Nice Alarm to the Invention Convention® this year. You promised you'd match whatever I earn to help me get there. You won't break that promise too, will you?"

Mom and Dad exchanged glances.

"Dad, did you lose one of your jobs again? I mean, you guys *are* still going to match what I earn, aren't you?"

"Of course I didn't," Dad answered. "Of course we are. Money is tight, but . . ."

"But . . . ?" I was almost afraid to hear the answer. Because of cutbacks, Dad had lost his position teaching philosophy at the university last year. Now he taught part-time at three different community colleges, driving 150 miles each day as he zipped from campus to campus in his Caddie convertible to make his classes on time. No wonder he always looked rumpled.

"A deal's a deal," Dad said. "Whatever you earn, we'll match it."

I sneaked a peek at Mom. She was massaging her head, but blinked in agreement.

"We know how important your inventions are to you," Dad went on. "That's what this whole thing's about. We're doing this to *help* you. So we've asked the principal at Patrick Henry to make an exception in your case. He's agreed—under two conditions." He ticked off on his fingers. "First, you need to join a club and take part in the scheduled activities for the rest of the year."

"What's the other condition?" I asked suspiciously.

Mom's kettle began to whistle, a shrill alarm of panic and impending doom.

"Your F in history," she answered. "You've got to bring that F up to a C by year's end, or else . . . or else take the class over in summer school."

FIVE

I WANTED TO rip off my clothes, throw myself on the floor, kick my feet, scream, cry, and flail a couple of spatulas until my parents saw the error of their ways.

But since that hadn't worked at the age of three (when Mom and Dad confiscated my Flip-a-Flapjack, the automatic pancake turner I'd created using rubber bands, a sandbox shovel, and a butane lighter), I doubted it would work any better now. Especially with the words "may not be socially mature enough" still ping-ponging against the kitchen walls.

So instead I just sat and stared at the meatloaf mummy on my plate. I knew exactly how he felt . . .

The doorbell rang.

"Saved by the bell," Mom murmured. She leaned close and kissed my forehead. "I know this is all a little unsettling, honey. We'll talk more tomorrow, all right?" She blew a kiss to Dad, then poured a steaming cup of tea. "I'm off to bed. Please don't disturb me. Not unless you're on fire or bleeding from the eyes." She shuffled away.

The bell rang again and again. In staccato dots and dashes. An urgent mayday.

"I'll do the dishes tonight," Dad offered, stacking the plates. "Why don't you let in your friends?"

I rose without a word. Moved jerkily to the front door.

"It's about *time*," Goldie said, flouncing into the hallway.

Hiccup hurried in behind her after tying Dasher and Dancer, his golden retrievers, to the porch rail.

Pierre followed with a sniff of disdain. "What eez that odor? Eet smells like"–he shuddered–"a loaf of meat."

Pierre fancies himself a world-class French chef (despite being less French than a poodle). When I didn't automatically offer him a gas mask, he dabbed at his nose with a white linen napkin flicked from his pocket. Then he took a blanketed bundle from his pack and laid it in my arms as gently as if it were a newborn baby. "Here eez zee electric beater. You will give her zee love she deserves, no? I am making zee meringue in home ec class tomorrow."

"Get us some sodas, Sneeze," said Goldie. She barreled up the stairs, disappearing through my bedroom door.

Pierre moved to hang his beret on a peg of Coat Away, thought better of it, and traipsed after her.

Hiccup peeked into the living room, his eyes glazing like donuts. "Where is *She?*" he whispered.

Hic's been in love with Mom ever since the day, when we were eight, that she made us grilled cheese sandwiches for lunch and Hiccup spied a particle of greenish mold on his cheddar and informed her he couldn't eat it because he might contract cheesewasher's lung–and she actually knew what that was.

"I have a token for Her," Hiccup revealed, slipping the

gift from his pocket. "It's a personal–*hic!*–ized petri dish."
Sure enough, etched across the plastic top in swirly, elegant letters: *Dr. Barbara Wyatt.*

I tried to praise Hiccup's present for Mom as "very scientific." All that bleated out was: "Bif-fik."

Hiccup peered into my face and said, alarmed: "What has *hic!* transpired?"

"I got a fish," I confessed.

"A . . . fish?" His eyes widened in horror.

In two hurried sentences, I told him about my parents' plans to skip me to ninth grade.

Hiccup's hics hit warp speed. "But *hic!hic!* you cannot *hic!hic!* go!"

"Hey, Sneeze," Goldie called down the stairs. "Where are those sodas? Oh, and Pierre wants a Perrier. With a twist of lemon."

I'll twist his lemon, I thought, but headed for the kitchen.

"Your parents *hic!hic!hic!* must be delusional. Has your dad been waxing his Cadillac with the garage door shut again?"

"No, but Mom's sick in bed, and–"

"She is ill?" Hiccup clenched my arm. "I must go to Her!"

He swooped up the stairs like Medicine Man on a Red Cross mission.

"Hic–wait–stop!" I dumped the beater on the couch and charged after him. "Mom doesn't want to be disturbed!"

The doorbell rang. Hayley.

"Dadcouldyoupleasegetthat?!"

Hiccup was raising his fist to knock on my parents' door. I've never been very good at baseball, but I did my best impression of a player sliding into home, skimming feet-first on my side along the polished hardwood floor, trying to clip Hic at the ankles.

I missed.

Hiccup twisted the doorknob and entered as I slid past him into the bathroom, crashing into the, uh, commode.

I scrambled up and hurried into Mom's room, bumping into the dark shape of Hiccup, whose fingers were poised above the light switch.

"Turn on that light," a hump grumbled from the bed, "and you're dead men."

Hic jerked his fingers away. "It is Hector, Mrs. Wyatt," he said in his most soothing bedside manner. "Hector *hic!hic!* Denardo. Can you tell me what is wrong? It is not the plague, is it?"

The hump sighed. "I'm 99.9 percent sure it's not the plague, Hiccup. But if it is, I promise you'll be the first to know."

"May I bring you a hot *hic!* water bottle for your feet?" he fussed. "A cool compress for your head? A humidifier with herbal-scented water?"

"Hiccup, sweet Hiccup," Mom said, "if you haven't gone away by the time I count three, I will surely rip out your liver. One . . . two . . ."

Hiccup and I plunged into reverse, backing into Goldie, who stood behind us in the hall, arms loaded with sodas.

"Geez, what a grouch!" she exclaimed. She craned her

neck to catch a glimpse of Mom as Hiccup pulled the door shut.

"Many diseases have emotional as well as physical ramifications," Hiccup lectured. "One should be more compassionate when the symptoms of a serious illness rear their ugly heads."

"Ooo, what kind of serious illness?" Goldie asked. I could practically see visions of future gossip columns dancing in her head.

"Just the flu," I said.

"Hmmph." She turned and stomped into my room.

Ace lay stretched in my old battered easy chair, reading the latest issue of *Invention Mania* magazine.

"Yo," he said, not looking up from the mag.

We were all shocked he'd shown up. But we'd learned never to question or make a fuss about Ace. If we did, he tended to vanish for days at a time. Last summer, after I found out his real name is John Smith (he uses Ace because it's more mysterious), he disappeared for six weeks.

Hayley sat on the floor next to Pierre, elbow resting on a bent knee. She winked in thanks for letting her join us.

My heart twisted.

Oh, man, how could I go to high school without her next year? She and Hic were the only ones who understood the way I felt about my inventions. Plus, maybe it was her Squint or something, but she had a way of looking at you that dared you to earn her friendship. And when you did, you knew she was worth it—because so were you.

"What's *she* doing here?" blurted Goldie, who didn't

like anyone impervious to informational blackmail.

"She's offered to be our, um, consultant," I answered.

"For putt-putt golf lessons?" Goldie smirked, handing out sodas.

"I got an A plus on my Egyptian project in Mr. Arnesen's class last semester," Hayley said coolly.

"Oh." Goldie flumped onto my bed, then began punching at the hidden treasure-lumps beneath my comforter. "Gad, what on earth do you sleep on, Sneeze. Turtles?"

"I think you'll be more comfortable over here," I said, guiding her to my desk chair. I took her place on the bed. "Let's get started. We've got lots to do tonight."

Goldie straightened with importance. "Since my mother is a principal, I say I should be the new chairperson of this group. What do you think?"

I thought it was a little like saying, "Gee, my dad is a doctor, so I am capable of amputating a gangrenous foot," but I kept my mouth shut.

So did everyone else.

Except for Hiccup, who was hicking. And Ace, who was snoring.

"Excellent," Goldie said, pulling her notebook from her pack. "Then I call this meeting to order. Our purpose tonight: To choose a *new and improved* project for the History Faire. Any suggestions?"

Pierre raised his hand. "I think we should prepare a sumptuous Egyptian banquet. Zee best way to zee judge's heart eez through his stomach, no?"

"Delicious idea," Goldie agreed, making notes in her large, loopy handwriting.

"I propose we study the ancient physician Imhotep," Hiccup put in, "the oldest known doctor in history. According to the Ebers papyrus, he practiced *hic!hic!* medicine around 2725 B.C., and–"

"Did he have zee cure for heeccups?" Pierre asked.

"There isn't a cure for heeccups, I mean hiccups," I answered, although for some reason gazing upon the beautiful face of my mother had *always* stopped Hiccup's hicking cold. Hadn't worked tonight, though. Strange . . .

"I concur," Hic said. "In extreme cases, surgery is the only option."

"Thanks for that *medicinal* idea," said Goldie, without writing anything down. "We'll definitely give it a lot of thought."

Hayley snorted. "Sure you will," she muttered. "*I* like your idea, Hic. What was that papyrus called again?"

Hiccup brightened. "The Ebers papyrus. It features 110 pages filled with 877 ancient remedies, including–"

Goldie wasn't listening. She was too busy bursting to tell us *her* idea. "I've been studying Egyptian fashions of that period," she announced, gesturing with the lavishness of a game show host, "and I think we should make authentic-looking costumes. Back then, men *and* women wore wigs and skirts and jewelry and makeup."

Pierre twisted his beret down low on his forehead. "I refuse to wear lipstick. No ifs, ands, or zee buts."

"And I," Hiccup began, "suffer from dermatitis, which–"

"OkayokayI'lltakethehint." Goldie drew a black line of curlicues through her notes. "Sneeze, any ideas that don't involve a feathered pharaoh?"

Hayley mouthed in confusion: *Feathered pharaoh?*

"In other words," Goldie continued, "any *good* ideas?"

I felt as if I'd been shoved against the wall. Hard.

King Cluck *had* been a good idea. The *best* idea. Or so I'd thought . . .

I gazed at the maze of shelves around my room that held dozens of my other "good" ideas. The gadgets had sat, untouched, gathering dust for months, like the treasures in a mummy's tomb. Lustrous shards of metal. Golden, jewel-like screws. Glittery cogs that hung in tinkling charms. All waiting for . . . what?

An inventor's afterlife.

What if I didn't have one? What if all my ideas laid an egg like King Cluck? What if I never had *any* ideas, ever again? Inventing wasn't just something I did. It was who I was. Without inventing, what would I do? What *could* I do?

"Sneeze!"

"Huh?" I turned and noticed Goldie as if for the first time.

She tossed her hair with melodramatic exasperation. "I *said*, any good ideas?"

I shook my head. "No," I answered, and my voice sounded far away. "No ideas at all."

SIX

HAYLEY SNORTED AND shot me an SOS à la mode: a Squint of Suspicion with a scoop of disbelief on top. There was no way around its meaning. *Of course you have an idea. You ALWAYS have an idea. So what aren't you telling me?*

I took a breath . . .

"Don't even *think* of opening your beak," Goldie warned. "And *you*"—she pointed at Hayley with her pen—"stop encouraging him."

"I haven't said a word," Hayley said in a calm voice.

Pierre broke in. "Allow me to explain. Sneeze has zee birdbrain idea to"—he gulped with distaste—"mummify a chicken!"

"A live chicken?" Hayley asked.

"No!" Pierre was aghast. "A dead chicken."

"A mummified chicken . . ." Hayley murmured. Then she laughed, once, a bright, triumphant sound like the sun bursting through clouds.

"It's brilliant!" She leaned forward with excitement. "Your other ideas—the banquet, the medicines—are good too, but Sneeze's is the best. I mean, there's so much you could do with a chicken mummy. You could prepare an entire burial chamber for him. Even paint a mural using hieroglyphics, telling stories about his great deeds."

Goldie rolled her eyes. "Yeah, like: 'Why did the Egyptian chicken cross the road? To get to the afterlife!'"

Pierre cracked up.

"The afterlife was no laughing matter to the Egyptians," Hayley said coolly. "*Nothing* was more important than their lives in eternity. Their whole culture was based on it. That's why Sneeze's idea is brilliant." She held my gaze as if to say: *You already knew that . . . didn't you?*

I pretended to have serious mechanical difficulties with my soda.

Goldie rapped the aquarium with her pen. "Let's take a vote. All in favor of doing Hiccup's project on I-Hop raise your hand!"

"*Imhotep,*" Hiccup corrected. "He was a physician, not a pancake restaurant."

"Whatever. Any takers?"

Hiccup's arm shot up.

Goldie made a big show of writing a paltry numeral 1 in her notes. "All those in favor of Pierre's Egyptian banquet . . . "

Pierre raised his arm with such seriousness, I felt like I should salute it.

Goldie swayed her arm like a palm tree in a hurricane, and prompted: "Ace?"

He shrugged, slipped the pencil from behind his ear, and drew a mustache on the cover girl of *Invention Mania*.

"Sneeze?"

Why not? At least when Pierre got through with a chicken, you could *eat* it.

I sighed and wiggled two fingers in a halfhearted "aye."

Hayley didn't even bother to snort. Those cold blue eyes of hers bored straight into mine, giving me an ice cream headache and a piece of her mind.

"It's unanimous," Goldie said, while Pierre swelled like a gloating toad. "We'll start our research tonight on Egyptian foods. We have only three weeks, so we gotta hustle."

"Have no fear, zee greatest of chefs eez here," Pierre announced. "You write zee reports, I shall do zee cooking."

"And to make our, uh, *consultant* happy," Goldie mock-bowed at Hayley, "let's prepare a funeral feast. Gee, anybody know what those dead guys used to eat?"

***

"Why didn't you stand up for your idea?" Hayley asked later that night, after the meeting ended. She, Hiccup, and I sat huddled outside on the top stone step of the front walkway, waiting for her dad. The cold April air soaked fast through my jacket and jeans like a spilled soda. But where my shoulder touched hers in one small nylon spot, it felt warm as summer.

I shrugged. "Why bother? Everyone except you two thinks my idea stinks. Besides, I have more important stuff on my mind . . ."

"I thought so," Hayley said, and waited.

"Speaking of things malodorous," Hiccup said, "tell her about the *hic!* fish."

"My mom and dad want me to skip eighth grade and start high school in September," I blurted. "They've worked it out with the principal and everything."

"Sneeze, that is so cool!" Hayley smiled into my eyes. "Congrats!"

I shook my head. "I don't want to go."

"And why not?"

"I have my reasons."

"And they are . . . ?"

I yanked a handful of popcorn-sized jasmine buds off a shrub and threw them one by one to the ground. Dasher and Dancer, who'd been nosing the grass while waiting for Hiccup, immediately gallumphed over, snuffling, hoping for something meat-like. When they realized the flowers weren't members of the beef, pork, or poultry family, they collapsed at my feet, panting, despondent.

"For one thing," I said, "I'd have to leave you and Hiccup."

Hayley shook her head. "You can't stay in middle school because of *us*!"

Hiccup hicked four distinct times, as if to say: *Oh! Yes! He! Can!*

"You're scared!" Hayley said. "Hey, don't worry. We'll still be your friends."

I was scared, all right. But not about losing her friendship. Not for *that* reason.

"Toss me another," Hayley said. "What other reasons you got?"

I told her about needing to bring my F up to a C. "I'll have to study constantly. Afternoons, nights, weekends. What if I don't have time for Gadabout?"

Hayley looked appalled. "But we need you! You're our best mechanic!"

Hiccup and I glanced at each other and laughed, remembering last summer when we'd applied together for jobs there. Back then Hayley thought *mechanic* was synonymous with *hoodlum*. She'd assumed we just wanted to throw after-hours swim parties in the Moat, snowboard down the plastic Alps, and tag the Great Pyramid with Day-Glo graffiti paint. It had taken us several weeks to prove ourselves otherwise.

"Sneeze is your *only* mechanic," Hiccup reminded her.

"True," Hayley admitted. "Daddy is hopeless when it comes to machinery."

"You fail to comprehend the severity of this situation," said Hiccup. "If Sneeze is unable to put in enough hours at Gadabout, his financial resources will evaporate, forcing him to—"

"Cancel the Invention Convention®," Hayley finished. "Listen, Sneeze, that's not gonna happen again. I won't let it happen. You helped Daddy and me so much last year when Gadabout was going under. All those great ideas for getting more people to play golf—"

"But Hayley, I don't want—"

"Now it's my turn to help *you.*" Chin tipped high, Hayley gazed into the night. "It's a fair trade. Your best for mine. I'll help you study while you're at Gadabout. Then you can go to the convention, and to high school, and—"

"Hayley," I said, "you're not listening to me. I don't *want* to go to high school."

"Then *tell* your parents."

"*She* will understand," Hiccup murmured, eyes dreamy.

No way. For the first time ever, Mom and Dad were downright giddy to giggling about my inventions. They bragged to everybody about me: the neighbors, the mailman, bank tellers, even wrong numbers! That's why our dining table looked like a waiting room for "sick" gadgets and appliances.

No, I couldn't tell them. They'd gone through so much to get me into Patrick Henry. If they knew the truth, they might not respect me anymore. They'd be disappointed. Angry.

And so might Hayley.

There had to be a way I could slip gracefully out of this predicament without letting on that I couldn't invent anymore.

But how?

"That you, Steve Wyatt?"

Dancer and Dasher leaped into Red Alert. I glanced up to see a man ambling along the sidewalk, holding a leash. Attached to the leash was what looked to be a large rat wearing a sweater.

D & D licked their muzzles and quivered. I knew they were thinking: *Meat!*

Hiccup grabbed their collars. The dogs strained and whined to get loose.

"That you, Steve?" I recognized our neighbor Mr. Rose. "The wife phoned earlier. Bitsy Boo's electric pajamas are on the blink. Can you lend us a hand?"

Geez, could I sink any lower? A repairman for chihuahua sleepwear!

Still, I forced myself to answer: "Sure, Mr. Rose. I'll get to it tomorrow."

"Wonderful!" he boomed. "Bitsy Boo, thank the nice wittle boy, won't you?"

Bitsy Boo closed his eyes and emitted a squeak.

D & D whined and strained harder, pulling Hiccup to his feet. They'd translated the squeak to mean: *Talking meat!*

Bitsy Boo took one shivery look at them and peed on the sidewalk.

"I think this is *the* opportune moment," Hiccup said, struggling to remain erect, "for me to take a leave of absence. On, Dasher! On, Dancer!" Grunt-hicking, he dragged the dogs in the opposite direction.

"Time for me to go too," Hayley said. "Here comes my dad."

Mr. Barker's old clunker clattered into the driveway. He beep-beeped the horn.

Hayley dove into the jasmine shrub.

"Lose another golf ball?" I asked.

"*She's* with him!" Hayley hissed. "The Girlfriend! How could he? He was supposed to pick me up *after* he took her home! He lied, just so I'd be forced to meet her!" The pungent shrub rustled with her anger. "I'm not going home with them. No way, José!"

The horn beeped again. The engine sputtered to a stop.

"He's getting out," I whispered. "What do you want me to do?"

"*Help.*"

Hayley didn't often ask for help. When she did, you knew she was Serious.

I vaulted off the steps, leaping out of the shadows and bumping into Mr. Barker halfway up the path.

"Sneeze, you startled me!" he cried, staggering back in a fake heart attack. "Sorry I'm late. Our movie ran long, so we came straight here. Is Hayley ready?"

"Um, not yet. Our meeting ran long too." I tugged at his arm, urging him back to the car.

"Did it, now? You kids sure are working hard on this project." He checked his watch. "It's almost ten—"

"We'll be done by ten-thirty, I promise. My dad will bring her home." I peeked around him, trying to catch a glimpse of the Girlfriend in the dark car.

"All right. Ten-thirty, but no later," Mr. Barker said. "Peach needs her personality sleep. If she doesn't get a full eight hours, come morning she's Little Miss Grump." He chuckled, the coins jingling in his pocket. He waved, and I hurried back up the walkway.

"Are they gone?" the shrub whispered.

"They're pulling away now."

"Did you see her? What does she look like?" Hayley eased herself out, raining jasmine.

"It was too dark for me to see much, but I think she had a ponytail."

"A ponytail!" Hands on her hips, Hayley snorted. "Who is he dating, a first grader? Maybe I can make some extra money babysitting her!"

"Come on," I said. "I'll get my dad to take you home."

"No, he shouldn't leave with your mom sick. I'll walk." She slung her pack onto one shoulder and marched down the steps.

"Hayley, you can't go home alone," I said, hurrying after her.

"Why not?"

"It's dark."

"So?"

"It's late."

"So?"

"So there could be, um, *mechanics* out there!" I grinned. She couldn't help herself. She grinned back.

"I'll walk her home," Ace said, emerging from behind a tree. It was a magic act I'd yet to get used to: him appearing and disappearing without any notice, without any trace.

"Hey, thanks, Ace," I said, trying to hide my surprise.

He shrugged. "Nuthin' else to do."

I wished I could say the same. Before bed I still had Pierre's electric beaters to fix—and a plan to hatch to keep myself out of Patrick Henry High.

SEVEN

BY FIVE A.M., I had formulated a plan. An ingenious plan. A desperate-times-call-for-desperate-measures plan.

I took out a blank journal and, by the moon-glow of my aquarium light, began writing The List of things to do that day.

Edison, Bell, and the Wright Brothers must've been struck with a rare form of aquatic shame, because they stayed hidden behind the plastic seaweed and the bubbly diver for the next hour.

"I don't like this any better than you do," I said, "but I don't have a choice."

I scribbled a few more items on The List.

The Nice Alarm changed its friendly *tick-tick, tick-tick* to a scolding *tsk-tsk, tsk-tsk*.

"Hey, give me a break," I defended. "I'm doing this for *you*. For *us*. It'll just be for a week or two. I promise." I slammed shut the journal. Jammed it into my pack. Threw on some clothes and headed for the kitchen.

Mom, swathed from neck to toe in a big nubby bathrobe, sat in her usual chair, sipping tea and eating soda crackers.

"Morning," she said with a pale smile that matched her eyes.

I dropped two pieces of bread into Nuts to You, the automatic peanut-butter-sandwich-on-toast-maker I'd invented. "Feeling better?" I asked.

"A little," she said, and cleared her throat. "Would you like to talk now, honey? About your transfer to Patrick Henry?"

"I'd *love* to, Mom. But I need to fix Bitsy Boo's pj's before school. Maybe tonight?" I forced a big smile. In order for my plan to work, I had to act as excited as possible about my parents' decision.

So far so good. Mom took another sip of tea, humming a little over the rim of her cup. Then her eyes widened.

"Steve!"

I turned to find a mushroom cloud rising above Nuts to You. The room reeked of barbecued peanut butter.

"Yikes!" In a flash I pulled the plug and plopped the device into the soapy water in the sink. It hissed and burbled, and sank like a safe. Rats. I'd yet to figure a way to keep the melted peanut butter from igniting on the toaster grill.

"Sorry, Mom," I said.

She took one bleak peek at the seared oily sludge, gulped, and zipped into the bathroom.

"At least this time I didn't set the curtains on fire!" I called after her.

No response.

I de-gunkified the sink and tossed the blackened Nuts

to You in the trash. Then I knocked on the bathroom door. "Mom, you okay?"

"Define 'okay,'" she said in a feeble voice.

"Okay enough that I can leave?"

"Yes. Just make sure you tell your dad you're going."

"DAAAAAAAAAAA-AAAAAD!" I screamed. "I'M LEAVING NOW!"

Mom cracked the door and glared at me with a slitted eye. "I meant, go upstairs *and tell him*. Scream like that again, and I'll ground you till you're sixty-four." The door clicked shut in my face. "Oh, and don't forget to sign up for a club at noon," added her muffled voice. "The principal said there's a list of them posted in the Student Activities office."

Rats. I'd forgotten about the club-joining requirement. But maybe this would work to my advantage. Maybe a prim and proper club would be another perfect place for me to carry out my plan . . .

I hooked on my tool kit, grabbed my pack, blew my nose with determination, and marched out to seize (and sneeze) the day.

***

"How is She feeling this *hic!hic!* morning?" Hiccup asked when we met at our lockers before first period.

"Better," I said. "Your gift really cheered her up."

My friend's freckles flushed with pleasure.

I took out my biology book. Then, thinking of The List, shoved it back into my locker and clanged the door. "You've got the hiccups awfully early today," I said.

"For your information," Hiccup announced, "these hiccups are the same ones I acquired yesterday in"—he shudder-hicked—"Fierce's class."

"You're kidding me, right?" Sure, Hic gets hiccups a lot. But I'd never known one of his episodes to last more than a few minutes. Being forced to sing in front of the class must've humiliated him even more than I'd thought.

"I speak with all honesty," he vowed, flashing Medicine Man's hand sign for TJV: Truth, Justice, and Vitamins for All.

"And because you're so honest, I need to warn you." I lowered my voice. "I've thought of a plan."

"What kind of plan? I am at your disposal, as always, of course!"

"Shhhhh, not so loud!" I swooped him into the alcove of a drinking fountain. "My plan will crash and burn if anyone suspects what I'm up to. Now listen: I've thought of a way to stay at Jefferson next year. But I think it's best if I keep you in the dark about the actual details."

"After all we've been through?" Hiccup asked. "We have never kept secrets from each other. We have a *hic!-hic!* history."

Hic and I had been best friends since that first day of kindergarten when he heard me sneeze about 147 times. *In a row.* He'd hurried over afterward, hand outstretched with a tissue, and said: "Hel–*hic!*–lo. My name is Hector. I've had croup, strep throat, and roseola. Twice. Would you like to play?"

"Hic, that's exactly why I can't tell you what's going on. Everyone knows we're like this." I pretzeled two fingers together. "You're the first person they'd interrogate. I don't want to put you, or my plan, in jeopardy by telling you more than you need to know. So no matter what happens in the next week, you're clueless, okay? As far as you're concerned, I'm just the same old Sneeze. Nothing's new. Nothing's changed. Got it?"

"Got it."

I sighed, and flashed the TJV. "I knew I could depend on you."

"And I, you," he responded. "And I am grateful for your concern. Under torture, I would experience an embarrassing case of involuntary micturition."

"Um, yeah," I agreed, figuring I'd look up that word in English. "C'mon."

I glanced from left to right before crossing the hall to our class. I caught a glimpse of Goldie, a few feet away, gossip notebook in hand. She peered at us, eyes agleam, pen poised. When she noticed I'd seen her, she ducked behind a soda machine.

"Uh-oh," I muttered. "Just act normal, okay? I mean, just be yourself."

Attached to a noisy clot of kids, we moseyed into class and took our seats.

Goldie slipped in soon after, face hidden behind her mane in a failed attempt at the old ostrich-head-buried-in-the-sand trick.

Hayley zipped in with a second to spare before the warning bell rang. She winked at me. I noticed her eyes were smudged underneath, like she was one of those crazy people (ahem) who stay up all night plotting fiendish plans.

I wondered if she'd been worrying about her dad and the Girlfriend.

Or worse, fuming about me not wanting to go to Patrick Henry next year.

A paving of hot shame steamrollered up my face. Man, if I thought she was mad at me before, just wait till the end of class. Hayley hated the kind of stuff I was about to do.

Mrs. Kasai, our biology teacher, hurried in. I felt the steamroller backing up, ready for another run. How could I do this to her? Mrs. Kasai was my favorite. We both loved the movie *Time Bandits,* and once spent an entire lunch hour reciting the funniest lines. Sometimes, she'd even call me Benson, the wacky assistant from the film who always wore a plastic raincoat—indoors.

Please don't let her call me Benson today!

For a split of a split-second, I almost scuttled my plan. Instead, I pushed that hesitation off a mental cliff. There could be no exceptions. I *had* to do this. There was no other way out.

I double-checked The List, memorizing the first page, then eased it back into my pack. The last bell rang. Mrs. Kasai started roll. When she called my name, I swallowed at the small, dry rodent caught in my throat. Then I shouted "Not here!" and there was no turning back . . .

***

For the rest of that morning, I became the reason some educators retire after only seventeen minutes of teaching, and take up something less stressful, like bomb defusing.

In Mrs. Kasai's class I gazed with desperation at the

57

clock every five minutes—as if to say: *Isn't this class* ever *going to end?!*—and sighed. Heavily.

Every three minutes I "accidentally" knocked my pack off my desk. Heavily.

Whenever a kid asked Mrs. Kasai a question, I'd ask, in blissful ignorance, the exact same question one minute later. Whenever Mrs. Kasai asked the class a question, I would wave my arm like I was stranded on a desert island, signaling the rescue aircraft, and yell: "I know! I know!" Then mumble, when she called on me, "Never mind."

It was Mrs. Kasai's turn to sigh. Heavily.

The pièce de résistance was when we were dissecting frogs and I impaled mine with an X-Acto knife, can-canning it across Mrs. Kasai's desk.

The class cracked up, and I spent the rest of that period in the hall. Ooo-la-la.

In Mr. Gomez's Spanish class, I discovered musical talents I never knew I had. I tapped my foot. Cracked my knuckles. Clicked my fingernails against my desk like castanets. Did drum rolls on the head of the kid in front of me with a pencil. Zipped and unzipped my jacket to the rhythm of "La Cucaracha."

And spent the rest of *that* period in the hall too. Olé!

Poor Mrs. Tibbits. I felt the worst about her. She'd been teaching literature at Jefferson since practically before the war (the Civil War, that is), and treated all her students like her dearest great-great-grandchildren: patting us sweetly on the cheek when we got a right answer; serving milk and homemade cookies on everyone's birthday; proudly showing us her "family" scrapbooks (pictures of every student she'd ever taught since her first day out of teachers college).

But that day, I was surely scratched off her cookie list forever when I popped like gunshot a wad of bubble gum the size of a watermelon, almost giving her a heart attack . . . tipped farther and farther back in my chair till it fell over with a deafening crash . . . then read aloud the part of Shakespeare's Hamlet in the voice of Porky Pig.

"Perhaps, dear," she said, her words quivery, "it would be best, dear, if you spent the rest of the hour in the hall."

"Ahbehdee, ahbehdee . . . that's all, folks!" I cried, scurrying from the class.

I barely had time to lean against the wall and grin with the thrill (and agony) of victory, when Hayley hustled out after me.

"I've got a three-minute bathroom pass," she said, arms folded, her face so close to mine, I was seeing double SOS's. "So start talking, buster. You've got some serious explaining to do."

EIGHT

"WHAT ARE YOU talking about?" I pumped my words full of light, fluffy innocence.

Unfortunately, Hayley's a girl who recognizes hot air when she hears it.

She snorted. "I'm talking about the way you've been acting all morning."

"How have I been acting?"

"So . . . so . . . *immature.*"

"You think I've been acting immature?"

She crossed her arms. "Yes, I do."

I let out a whoop of delight. "Thank you, Hayley! *Thank you!*" I tap-danced in a whirling circle around her, then, without thinking, grabbed her by the shoulders and gave her a great big kiss on the lips.

On the lips.

A kiss.

A great big one.

YIKES!I'DJUSTGIVENHAYLEYAGREAT-BIGKISSONTHELIPS!!!!!!!!!!!!!!!!!!!!!!!!!

"Oops," I said.

"Ha ha!" I said.

"Sorry," I said.

I expected her to spit or gag or go in search of Hiccup to borrow his pocket-sized bottle of antibacterial soap and maybe a wire scrub brush. Instead, she got this scrinched, confused look to her eyes, and touched her mouth with her fingertips, as if her lips belonged to somebody else.

"That's . . . okay," she said at last.

We just stood there, gazing at the floor. At least, I think it was the floor. Most schools have floors, don't they? You know, that hard stuff under your feet that you walk on . . .

"What were we talking about?" I asked.

Just then, Goldie burst out of Tibbits's classroom and skidded to a stop. She held her *Goldie's Gossip* notebook in one hand, tape recorder in the other, and a hall pass in her mouth. When she saw us, she tried to jam everything into the pockets of her jumpsuit.

"Um, herro," she mumbled around the hall pass. "Muzzup?"

"What are *you* doing out here?" Hayley asked coolly.

Goldie took the hall pass from her mouth and waved it under Hayley's nose. "Bathroom," she said.

"Is there a convention in the girls' bathroom that I don't know about?" I asked.

"Do you always take your tape recorder to the bathroom?" Hayley asked.

Goldie glanced down to see the microphone cord coiling out of a pocket. Her faced reddened. Hand over hand she reeled in the cord, then edged backward.

"Ste-phen Wy-att," she singsonged. "I know you're up to something. And I'll find out what it is. I always get my *information!*" She flounced down the hall.

61

"See, even *she* noticed," Hayley said. "So do you want to explain to me what it is you're doing you won't admit you're doing and why?"

It took me a few seconds to translate what she'd said. Then I answered: "I can't right now. You know Goldie is a master of disguise. She could be impersonating a locker, a soda machine, eavesdropping as we speak."

"Huh," Hayley said. "Fine. I'll expect an explanation at lunch, in a Goldie-free zone of your choice." She moved to open Tibbits's door.

I sighed. I'd be joining a school club at lunch. If everything went according to plan, I wouldn't have to do any explaining until my problem was solved and—

"Wait a second." Hayley stopped, hand on the knob. "You were *happy* when I said you'd been acting immature." She shot an extra-strength SOS into my eyes. "Why would you purposely act like a two-year-old? Why would you purposely bug your teachers to the point where they'd kick you out of class?"

She stopped. She gasped. She grabbed my pack and unzipped it.

"Hey!" I shouted. "Get outta there!" I yanked on the shoulder strap.

"Where is it?" she demanded, yanking back.

We tug-of-warred a few more times. "Where's what?"

Hayley snorted. "Playing dumb won't work with me. I know your IQ. You're writing a sequel, aren't you? *101 Ways to Bug Your Teacher!*"

"What?!" My jaw did a dramatic bungee jump, springing back with a snap.

A janitor in work boots clumped by and stared at us, his large broom making a whiskery sound as he pushed it along the hall.

Hayley's voice dropped low and serious. "You are, aren't you?"

"I swear I'm not—"

"Only this book isn't at all like the first one. *101 Ways to Bug Your Parents* was clever. Funny. You got kids to notice things they accidentally do to their parents. It made us laugh because we saw ourselves on every page. It helped us let off steam. Helped *me* let off steam."

"Hayley—"

Her lips hinted a smile. "Sometimes, when Daddy goes on and *on* about 'Daisy this' and 'Daisy that,' I want to cram golf balls into my mouth to keep from screaming. And then I remember your book . . ." She raised her chin and stared through me, the way she does when she's thinking about her mom. "That's when I go to my secret place, where Mom and I used to play. I hide in there and read about doing number forty-three. Or eighty-seven." She grinned past me. "It makes me feel so much better . . . "

She shook her head as if to erase the memory. The golf ball earrings swung so hard, they looked like they were teeing off.

"But in this new book, Steve," she went on, "the things you're doing are just plain rude. Mean."

Her words stung fierce and hot, like I'd thrust my heart into a buzzing wasp nest. I rubbed at my chest, but you can't massage away the truth. I *had* been acting rude. Mean. But it was the only way . . .

"Hayley, I'm *not* writing a sequel, okay?" I said. "I swear I'm not. So just give me my pack, and go back into class."

She released the strap. "First tell me what's going on."

"I'll tell you at lunch."

"This isn't like you at all."

"Yes, it is," I said in defiance. "This is the *real* me. I'm a punk. A brat. A hoodlum. Far too immature to go to high school and—"

Oops.

"*That's* why you're wreaking havoc in class?" Hayley's words overflowed with surprise. "So your teachers will say you're not mature enough to skip eighth grade? Steve, this is ridiculous! Just tell your mom and dad you don't *want* to go to Patrick Henry next year!"

"I can't." My voice sounded hollow, dull. "And I can't tell you why I can't, so don't ask, okay?"

Her squinty expression asked anyway.

Because, I answered to myself. Because I'd rather have you think I'm a bratty, rude, immature punk than to know I can't invent anymore . . .

"Okay," Hayley said, "if that's the way you want it." She shoved her hands into her pockets. "But don't you dare pull any of that immature hoodlum stuff at Gadabout, do you hear? 'Cuz if you do, I'll fire you so fast, it'll knock your socks off—with your shoes still on."

I almost choked. "Hayley! I would *never.* Gadabout is my *home.* You know I wouldn't—I couldn't. I *swear.*"

"Huh. See you at lunch." Hayley disappeared into Mrs. Tibbits's room without a backward glance.

NINE

FOURTH PERIOD, ART class.

Michelangelo . . . da Vinci . . . Vermeer . . . and Mr. Hunter's amazing whistling nose.

Some days his breathing is a symphony. Others, a polka. Today, as Mr. Hunter rhapsodized about Picasso, the Nose performed a soothing lullaby at 28 WPM (Whistles Per Minute), and I started to feel dozey.

Must . . . stay . . . AWAKE.

I struggled to look alert. Mr. Hunter considers it a personal insult if a student even stifles a yawn in his class.

Besides, I had work to do.

I slipped my journal from my pack and propped it open inside my art history book. Then I turned to the first page:

101 Ways to Bug My Teachers
(A Work-in-Progress)
by Stephen J. Wyatt
PRIVATE AND PERSONAL
NO TRESPASSING
THIS MEANS YOU!!!!!!

I hadn't lied to Hayley. This wasn't a sequel. It wasn't

a book. It was only a simple list. A list for me and for me only . . .

I ticked through the "ways" I'd used so far. Rats. Only a few left of the eighteen I'd concocted last night. Not even close to enough for Hunter's class, because what I *did* have left, I needed for world history with Fierce. I was 99.99999 percent sure Ms. Pierce was the teacher who'd said I was not "socially mature enough" to attend Patrick Henry High. I planned to use that to my advantage, even if it meant spending all of fifth period tossing dice for the Death Roll.

Meanwhile, I needed to needle Mr. Hunter.

But how?

Breathe, whistle. Breathe, whistle . . .

"If someone will turn off the lights," Mr. Hunter said, "I'll show slides of Picasso's finest pieces now."

I gave a mental groan, pinched open my eyelids, and read through The List again. It was time to take stock of what I'd done so far. Scientists didn't just gather information. They analyzed and evaluated it too.

I dug out a pencil, and in the twilight of the slide show, organized the "ways" I'd tested that morning. I used the same three categories I'd created while researching *101 Ways to Bug Your Parents*: Duds, Dynamos, and Disasters.

Duds caused teachers to merely frown, flinch, or ignore me.

Dynamos provoked them to sputter, stutter, or send me into the hall.

Best-case scenario? Getting sent to the principal's

office and having him call my parents.

Breathe, whistle. Breathe, whistle . . .

Chewing bubble gum in Mrs. Tibbits's class? Definitely a Dud, dear. She hadn't batted an eye until I started snap, crackle, and popping the wad as loud as her arthritic joints. Then it became a Dynamo.

Snap, crackle, and popping my knuckles in Mr. Gomez's class? El Dud, for sure. He hadn't gone totally loco until I cracked my knuckles *and* clicked my finger-nails *and* tapped my foot in a one-man mariachi band. Then: Ay, caramba! Dynamo City.

Breathe, whistle . . .

I nibbled on my eraser.

Timing and frequency. Those were the keys. *When* or *how many times* you did something buggable were often more important than *what* you actually did.

And some of the *whats* worked best in combinations. Not everyone grew annoyed at the same things. The trick was knowing my teachers' pet peeves so well that I could predict their reactions: Dud-ly, Dynamic, or Disastrous.

Disasters, such as getting suspended or expelled, had to be avoided at all costs.

Worst-case scenario? My plan falling into the wrong hands.

Or everyone learning that my buggable personality was fake.

Breathe, whistle. Breathe, whistle . . .

Man, it's awfully warm in here . . .

Before I remembered I shouldn't, I stretched and yawned.

Mr. Hunter rewarded me with a throat-drilling *HARRUMPH*.

I smiled into The List.

I knew Mr. Hunter very, very well.

Slouching lower into my chair, I thunked my feet up onto my desk and yawned again. Vigorously.

"Mr. Wyatt," Mr. Hunter demanded, "are we keeping you up?"

"You sure are," I admitted with a grin, and slid straight into dreamland . . .

***

I had a refreshing catnap—until Mr. Hunter kicked me into the hall 17.5 seconds later, that is. (*Awright!* Sneeze: 4. Teachers: 0.) Then, as soon as the lunch bell rang, I zipped into the Student Activities office. I needed to continue with my plan, and that meant finding a club to join.

As Mom had mentioned, I found a list, tacked to a bulletin board, of clubs still taking members. I ran my finger down the paper.

Glee Club.

I didn't know what that was, but since I hadn't experienced much glee lately, I decided to pass.

Photography Club.

Ha. Dad hadn't let me near his expensive photo stuff since the day I'd invented Pictures Ahoy, a dry-land-to-underwater-camera conversion kit. I'd tested it in my aquarium, using Dad's Nikon, where Bell got stuck inside the lens for three days.

Inventor's Club.

Whoa!

I did a double take. Then a triple. My heart sputtered and drubbed like the world's first internal combustion engine.

An inventor's club. A club for people *just like me*. I hadn't even known it existed. Maybe I *had* been too antisocial, too busy with Gadabout and my own inventions.

With a pen, I scribbled the room number on my hand and thudded up the stairs, the chug of my heart propelling me faster, forward.

The club would be perfect for me. Not only could I fool Mom and Dad and the principal that I was taking this club-joining thing seriously, but maybe I *could* take it seriously. Maybe talking to other inventors—kids who felt like they were walking around naked unless they had crescents of grease rimming their fingernails . . . kids who'd rather spend an afternoon at a hardware store than at Disneyland . . . kids who when finding a lone bolt gleaming on the sidewalk thought only of contraptions to come—was just what I needed to blow my inventor's block to smithereens.

I found Room 201. A handmade sign thumbtacked to the door read *I've Got An Idea: The Inventor's Club.*

Odd, I thought, feeling a niggle of suspicion in the back of my brain. I've Got An Idea, Inc. was the name of my fictitious company. Hiccup and Ace were the only people who knew I used that name on stationery, listing myself as "president" when writing to novelty companies about my inventions. I didn't want the bigwigs to know I was a kid. I'd always assumed kid-inventors were rare, so I doubted grown-ups would believe I had talent.

But if there were others like me . . .

I ignored my suspicions. Reached for the doorknob. Twisted it. Strode inside, ready to hail a room full of fellow inventors-in-arms.

Instead, sitting at the teacher's desk, I saw only July Smith—Queen of the Clubs—and perched before her, like ladies-in-waiting, the Amys. The rest of the seats were empty.

"It's a *boy*," said the Amys.

"So it is," the Amys said.

The Amys are two eighth-grade girls named—you guessed it—Amy. Once upon a time they must've had last names, but no one remembers those now. They've been best friends for so long, it's like they've morphed into one person.

"He's wearing a holster," said the Amys.

"Are you a cowboy?" the Amys asked.

"The Western Club is down the hall, Room 208, if you hurry you can still sign up for the field trip to the rodeo on Saturday, talk to Tony Sandoval, the club advisor, bus leaves at eight a.m. sharp, permission slips available in the Student Activities office," July said, without glancing up, without taking a breath. She sat studying notes on a clipboard while entwining her hair into one long French braid.

"Um, I'm not a cowboy. I'm an inventor." I pulled my screwdriver from its, uh, *holster*, as proof.

"What's *that?*" asked the Amys, looking alarmed.

Did I mention the Amys share everything, including one lone brain cell?

My high expectations ejected like a pilot from a crashing fighter jet. I turned to leave, scrubbing my nose in disappointment. It had begun to tickle.

And tingle.

And itch.

"Ahhhhhhhh-CHOOO!"

"He sneezed," said the Amys.

"Is that what that was?" the Amys said.

I heard a pencil click to the floor. "Wait a minute, don't move, don't leave," July said, her voice urgent. "Are you Sneeze Wyatt? Inventor of the Nice Alarm?"

Surprised, I blew my nose in affirmation. Not everyone knew about the alarm. "You've heard of it?"

"It's a legend at my house, I've even heard of your company, and I borrowed the name for our new club." July glided toward me, her chocolate-colored cape rippling like the wings of a stingray. She offered a weird smile that lifted one corner of her mouth but never reached her eyes, and took my hand in her cool fingers, leading me to a chair. She smelled like vanilla. "Did you come to join, I hope so, because we need four to enter, and with *you* I know we can win."

"'Four' what?" I asked. "'Enter' what? 'Win' what?"

"Four inventors, the local Invention Convention, two thousand dollars," July replied. She jerked a neon-yellow flyer off the bulletin board and held it out, staples still clinging for dear life to its edges.

I skimmed the flyer, which read:

LEMON COUNTY SCHOOLS
INVENTION CONVENTION° CONTEST
OPEN TO ALL MIDDLE AND JUNIOR HIGH SCHOOL INVENTORS' CLUBS
FIRST PRIZE: $2,000
LOCAL WINNERS WILL BE ENTERED
IN THE STATE FINALS
STATE WINNERS WILL ATTEND
THE NATIONAL INVENTION CONVENTION°–
ALL EXPENSES PAID

There was smaller print at the bottom, but my brain was stuttering: "T-two th-thousand dollars . . . ?"

"Of course, the award would be noted on our permanent records," July was saying. "That's important if you're trying to get a scholarship for a decent private high school."

I wasn't listening.

This is it. My chance to go to the national convention, without Mom and Dad's help. I could win the local and state contests, I knew I could. Soon I'd be winging my way to national, where I'd sell the Nice Alarm to the highest bidder. Then the floodgates of inventing would burst open in my brain again . . .

"How do I join your club?" I asked.

"You just did," July said, glancing at her watch, gliding to the front of the room, gathering up her clipboard and an armload of notebooks. "I've got oodles of other club meetings this hour, so I need to go. Could you bring the alarm to the meeting Friday, at noon. I think it's important that we get a look at it right away so we can prepare our entry."

"Of course—"

"Great." Again, the half smile. "Oh, I forgot to tell you, I'm July Smith, president of the club, and this is Amy and Amy, our vice presidents, you can be secretary or treasurer or flag bearer, whatever you want, just as long as we get our entry in on time, the deadline is Friday!" She sailed out the door, leaving a whiff of vanilla in her wake.

"Could you show us that whatchamacallit again?" asked the Amys.

"You mean the screwdriver?" I held it out, handle forward in the safest prescribed method.

"Oooo," whispered the Amys. "It's cute."

"So is he," the Amys whispered back.

TEN

I ESCAPED THE Amys before they started *oohing* and *aahing* and *hey-what-is-that?-ing* about my wrench and pliers, then raced to the caf to buy a burger. Lunch would be over in ten minutes. I wasn't hungry, but maybe the pinballs ricocheting in my stomach would do so more gently if there were bits of bread in there to cushion the blows.

The bun stuck to the roof of my mouth. Even with gobs of ketchup and gulps of milk to help, I felt like I was trying to swallow a loaf of sawdust. Finally, I lobbed the burger into the trash. I would have to face Fierce on an empty stomach.

Ace lounged outside the classroom, cleaning his nails with a toothpick, while other students pushed inside. Ace always manages to be the last kid into class—at least ninety seconds after the stragglers—like he's doing the teacher a huge favor by showing up. Like showing up is an after-afterthought.

"Yo," he said.

"Hey, Ace. Got your research notebook started?"

He arched an eyebrow as if to say *oh, puh-leeze,* and resumed his manicure.

"Um, sorry," I said. "What was I thinking?"

Pierre appeared at my elbow.

"Eez she done?" he asked, wringing his hands.

"Of course not," I answered, trying to arch a brow as coolly as Ace had done. "Fierce said we were to have *started* our notebooks by today."

"No, you idiot! Not zee notebook, zee electric beater! You fixed her, no?"

"Oh! Yeah." I opened my pack. "Her motor—I mean, *its* motor—was about to burn out. I replaced it." *At two a.m.,* I should've added.

"Gently, gently," Pierre warned, as I laid the beater in his arms. "Come to papa!" He turned his back without a thank-you, crooning to the cuddled bundle.

Hiccup hurried to my side. "What a relief to find you hail and hardy!" he exclaimed. "Your absence was metic–*hic!*–ulously noted by Hayley and me during the luncheon hour."

"I'm sorry to have worried you, pal. My parents made me join a club, remember? I, uh, just forgot to tell you guys I'd have to do it during lunch."

"*You* joined a *club*?!" Goldie's face popped over Hiccup's shoulder. "So you *are* up to something! Come on. Tell me." Her fingers crept toward her notebook. "I can keep a secret. Honest."

Hiccup, Pierre, and I looked at each other and burst out laughing.

"Well, I *can*," she insisted, stamping a foot. "You might as well tell me. I'll find out soon enough, anyway. I always do."

"Nothing's going on, Goldie," I assured her, fighting to

keep my voice steady. "You're h-hallucinating."

"But your irrational behavior of this morning . . ." Hiccup put in.

I arranged my face into what I hoped was a sincere and puzzled expression. "What are you talking about? I haven't been acting any different than I usually do. *I'm the same old Sneeze, remember?*" I used the words to nudge him as hard as I could without Goldie noticing.

At last the sun rose in Hiccup's eyes. "Oh. *Hic!* Oh! *Hic! OOOOOOH . . .*"

The warning bell rang.

"Time for class," Goldie said in a bossy tone. "Are your notebooks ready for inspection? I think Fierce will like our feast idea a whole lot better than the scheme *someone,* ahem, hatched yesterday."

She strode through the door. Pierre followed, beater tucked under one arm.

I took a deep breath and let it out slowly. Now or never . . . Do or die . . .

Die. The singular of *Dice.* As in the *Death Roll.*

I shook my head like a dog after a bath, hoping to fling off the thought, and plunged into the classroom.

Hiccup grasped my arm, yanking me back into the hall.

"Sssneeze!" he hissed.

"What's the matter?" His face had blanched fish-belly white, like yesterday while singing "Old MacDonald."

"I cannot go in *hic!hic!hic!* there."

"Why not?"

"Because . . ." His fingers still gripped me as tightly as

76

a machinist's pipe jaws. "Because I have an inkling of *hic!hic!hic!* your Plan. Do not enact it, Sneeze. Not in there. Please. Otherwise, Fierce will *hic!hic!hic!* Fierce will *hic!hic!hic!–*"

He couldn't finish the sentence. His hiccups kept marching like an army of goose-steppers.

"It's the only way, Hic," I said. "I have to."

He shook his head and released my arm. "I cannot watch, my friend. I cannot *hic!hic!hic!* bear to watch what she will do to you . . ."

Shudder-hicking, he backed away.

"Hector!" I was shocked at how much this upset him. I'd never seen him hiccup like this before. Never seen him so *scared* before. "Hector, it won't be bad. I promise. It *won't*. Hey–where are you going?"

"Tony's. Need to *hic!hic!hic!* lie down. Shall try to come back *hic!hic!hic!HIC!*" He scurried toward the nurse's office.

I started to go after him–then stopped. Tony could calm him better than I could, right? And if Hic really *was* as freaked as he looked, it'd be better for him *and* for me if he sat out fifth period.

I sighed and turned, catching a glimpse of Ace watching us both like a cat at a mouse hole. Our eyes locked for an instant, then he plucked an imaginary hair off his shirt–but not before I saw his brow wrinkle in what looked like a furl of concern.

Could he be as worried about Hiccup's reaction as I was?

Naw. Ace was too cool to worry about anything.

The final bell rang.

Kids ran. Doors slammed. The hall fell silent.

I waited ninety seconds, then bowed to Ace and said: "After you."

Ace shrugged, opened the door, and ambled inside. I waited another agonizingly long sixty seconds. Then, prepared to fight fire with fire, I glanced one last time at The List, and . . .

Fierce sat perched high atop The Tower, blazer buttoned to the neck, her red hair glowing like hot coals under the cold fluorescent lights.

"How kind of you to honor us with your presence this afternoon, Mr. Wyatt," she said. "Do you have a late slip?"

I pretended to think hard about her question before drawling: *"Nooope."*

With her pencil, Fierce made a black mark in the attendance book open on her lap. "The rest of Group Two has already turned in their notebooks, Mr. Wyatt. Do you have yours for me to peruse?"

"Nooope," I repeated. "My parents haven't finished doing it yet."

A girl giggled. A couple of boys cracked up. I grinned their way and waved.

"Very funny, Mr. Wyatt." Fierce extended her hand. "Your notebook, please."

"Uh, yeah, I got that somewhere . . ."

I opened my pack and dumped everything onto Fierce's desk: Books. Bus pass. Wadded tissues. Extension cord. Set of calipers. Allergy medicine. Keys to Gadabout. A dollar eighty, all in pennies.

Fierce tapped her fingernails against the attendance book.

"Oh, now I remember!" From my pocket, I dug out a tight triangle of paper.

"You folded the first page of your history notebook into a *cootie-catcher*?" Fierce asked, her voice rising from Simmer to Steam.

"It was the only way it would fit into my pocket," I explained.

A few more students cracked up.

Fierce shot the class a flame-thrower glance, but started to unfold the catcher. I scooped all my stuff back into my pack, and strolled toward my desk.

"Hold on, Mr. Wyatt. This is written in *purple crayon*."

"I didn't have a pencil," I said with a shrug.

"You will copy these notes over *now*. With *my* pencil," Fierce said, holding it out to me.

"Gee, thanks!" I grabbed the pencil and, gnawing on the eraser, slouched into my seat.

"Sacré bleu!" whispered Pierre, his beret awry from laughing. "Have you gone crazy?"

"As I was saying to Group Two," Fierce said, tossing the attendance book onto her desk. "The idea of a funeral feast is an interesting one. I've not seen it done before at the History Faire. Aside from the food, I'd like you to research the type of mourning clothes the family members would've worn at the feast and . . ."

As Fierce lectured on, I eased out of my seat, meandered up the aisle, crossed in front of her to the pencil sharpener, and began grinding way The sound was similar to a massive redwood being pulverized at a sawmill.

"*Excuse* me, Mr. Wyatt." Fierce's voice sizzled in the air above the din. "What do you think you are doing?"

"I can't hear you," I shouted.

"Stop sharpening that pencil. *Now.*"

"I can't hear you! Wait till I finish sharpening this pencil!" I ground away for a few more centuries till I had a stub the size of my thumb, then blew the shavings onto the floor.

"Mis-ter Wy-att," Fierce said, her voice rumbling now, a volcano ready to blow. *"Take a seat."*

"Where should I take it?" I asked.

That did it.

The class blew first, every kid melting in a spew of laughter.

Fierce's face flushed as red as her hair, red as hot coals.

"Death Roll," she pronounced.

Silence—except for a trickling titter from Goldie.

"Death Roll," Fierce repeated.

They were the words I had wanted and waited to hear. Still, a cold, bony hand seemed to grip my heart. I tried to breathe around the squeeze as I moved in jerks toward the Death Roll box.

The class held its collective breath. I picked up the dice, cupped and shook them in my palm, then flicked them onto Fierce's desk.

"Nine," she announced.

Oh, man, I thought, checking the chart. *No one* had ever rolled that number.

Number nine reads: *Dance the hula. IN COSTUME.*

Fierce pulled from behind her desk a grass skirt, pink plastic lei, and a bikini top made of coconut shells. With fumbling fingers, I tied the skirt and top over my jeans and T-shirt. The lei went on like a necklace.

"Ooo, baby," a boy shouted as I faced the class.

Someone wolf-whistled. My cheeks prickled, hot and sharp.

The class cracked up again.

Fierce snapped on a portable CD player. Wavy Hawaiian guitar music lilted into the air.

I hopped from foot to foot, like walking across a hot sidewalk. I waggled my arms, twiddled my fingers, trying to match the melody.

The class cracked up harder. Their faces were a blur. I could only focus on Pierre, who was clinging to his desk, half out of his chair (and half out of his mind) in a spasm of glee.

My nose tickled.

And tingled.

And itched.

"AAAAH-CHOOEY!"

The grass skirt floomped down around my ankles, and the coconut bra popped off. It clatter-skittered across the floor, stopping at the open door, where Hiccup now stood, wide-eyed, wide-mouthed.

He lowered his head to gaze at the bra touching his toes. Then he gazed at me, his face white and shiny and stretched, like an overblown balloon.

And I saw reflected in his face what he saw in mine: Humiliation. Embarrassment. Pain.

The "audience" howled.

"HIC!HIC!HIC!HIC!" Hiccup said. He turned and ran into the hall.

I took a step to run with him. To escape. To hide–

And stopped.

Maybe it was the sneeze that had cleared my head. Or maybe it was my friend's face, looking so tortured. Either way, I realized what I'd said to him before class was true. This wasn't so bad. In fact, it wasn't bad at all, because–

I didn't care anymore.

I didn't care kids were laughing at me. I didn't care what weird things they were thinking about me.

I only cared about my inventions and Gadabout and staying at Jefferson Middle School next year.

If that meant I had to dance, well, I would *dance.*

I wiggled back into the grass skirt and began to hoof it anew. Grinning with abandon, I shimmy-ed and samba-ed, mambo-ed and rumba-ed. The kids continued to roar. But now they were laughing *with* me, not *at* me. They were cheering and clapping too . . .

The music snapped off. Still laughing, I whirled to face Fierce. Her green eyes squinted, confused, as if not recognizing me, as if almost afraid of me.

Then they blazed with anger again, and she shouted: *"Principal's office. Now!"*

"Mahalo and aloha!" I said, tossing kisses and swishing my skirt as I hula-ed out the door, applause and cheers of "Encore! Encore!" escorting me in victory into the hall.

ELEVEN

THE SCHOOL SECRETARY barely blinked when I sashayed into the main office. Maybe she used to work in Hawaii, where something was wrong if a guy wearing a grass skirt *didn't* appear at her desk before three o'clock. In a soft, polite voice, she said: "Mr. Garrett will be with you in a few minutes. Please take a seat."

This time, I did *not* respond with: "Take it where?"

Instead, I plunked onto a hard chair, grinning like a jack-o'-lantern. So far, my plan had worked as well as a brand-new socket wrench. I hadn't expected to be sent to the principal so soon. If I kept this up for a week, tightening the "bolts" in every class, visiting Mr. Garrett every day . . .

The secretary's phone rang.

"I'm sorry," she said to me, replacing the receiver. "Mr. Garrett has been detained, and the vice principal is in a meeting." She wrote out a hall pass. "I'll let Ms. Pierce know by intercom that you're returning to class. You two will need to work out this, uh, tropical situation on your own."

Oh, golf tees, I muttered mentally, borrowing Hayley's favorite cuss word. Going back to Fierce would ruin everything.

Unless . . . I *didn't* go back.

I headed instead to Tony's office to check on Hiccup. I crossed my fingers that his hic attack had subsided. If not, I needed to show him I was okay so that *he'd* be okay.

I found Tony filling a jar of alcohol with thermometers that tinkled like icicles.

"He vamoosed 'bout five minutes ago," Tony said before I opened my mouth.

I sighed with relief. "Is he going to math?"

Tony frowned. "Nope. His mama picked him up. I thought he should see a doc." He closed a blue medical file that I figured was Hiccup's. "He was hickin' somethin' fierce. Looked awful, like he'd been ridden hard and put away wet. What in the name of the Alamo happened to that boy?"

"He didn't tell you?"

"Mum as a tombstone." Tony leaned back in his chair, legs stretched out on the desk, feet crossed at the booted ankles on top of Hic's file. "I suspect it's one doozy of a yarn. Care to spin it for me? Might do you some good."

I flashed on Hiccup's face: his eyes and mouth three horrible O's of shock and shame.

I shook my head, struggling to cap the guilt bubbling inside me. That was about as easy as putting a cork in an erupting volcano.

"So, Lulu from Honolulu, care to at least explain the getup?" Tony gestured at my luau ensemble.

"This old thing?" I jammed the grass skirt and lei into my pack. "Just something I threw on this morning."

"Uh-huh." He looked at me like he was waiting for

something more, like he was willing to wait as long as whatever that something would take.

I shifted my gaze from Tony's face to a CPR chart on the wall.

"Whatcha workin' on these days?" he asked. "You haven't brought a new invention by in I don't know how long."

That rat-of-a-secret squirmed.

I shrugged. "I—haven't had time to work on anything. I've been really busy with, you know, homework and stuff."

"Never known homework to stand in the way of your inventions before," Tony said, his voice quiet.

I cleared my throat. "Well, I'm not doing so well in history. And uh, I've had to do a lot of work for the neighbors and the kids at school. Fixing lawn mowers and dishwashers and computers . . ."

"Mmm," Tony said. He ambled over to help a girl who'd appeared at the door wearing PE clothes and a bleeding cut on her knee.

Relieved to be off the spot, I dropped into his chair, listening to Tony murmur words of TLC (Twangy Loving Care, I called it) as he swabbed the girl's knee with antiseptic. While he worked, I swiveled. I pretended to enjoy the spin, but I was actually hoping the breeze I created would accidentally blow open Hic's file so I could catch a clue about his condition.

No such luck.

Then I noticed a leather frame, peeping from behind a canister of cotton balls and a pile of first aid books. It held a faded photo of a cowboy riding a bull. The bull was kicking, back hooves slashing toward the sun. The cowboy, his back arched against a blurred background, rode with his right arm flung up, like he was waving to the sky.

I peered closer at the photo. There was something familiar about the rider's caterpillar eyebrows . . .

"Is this *you*?!" I blurted.

Tony glanced my way, then continued cleaning the girl's knee. "Sure is."

"I didn't know you rode in rodeos! I knew you were from Texas and all, but—"

"I was on the circuit for a spell," Tony said in a bored drawl. "Saddle bronc, bulldoggin', calf ropin'. You name it, I did it. 'Tony Macaroni'—that's what they called me."

The girl giggled.

"Tony Macaroni," I repeated with a laugh. "Did you ever win a trophy?"

Tony smoothed a large bandage on the girl's knee. "You don't win trophies in rodeos," he said. "Big gold belt buckles, that's the prize of cowboys. And yep, I won my fair share." With a slow smile and a "You take care now, hear?" he sent the girl on to PE.

I squinted even closer at the picture. I realized the blurred background was actually faces of cheering crowds. "Wow, you must've been good. Why'd you quit?"

"Too darn dangerous," he answered, soaping his hands in the sink.

"Lots of broken bones, huh?"

Tony shrugged. "Won my fair share o' those too. But

that's not what I'd call 'dangerous.' It was ridin' for the wrong reasons, that's where the danger was."

"I don't get it," I said.

Tony dried his hands on a paper towel. Plucked the photo from me. His chili brown eyes gazed into the picture, like he was staring at the young man he used to be.

"Sneeze," he said finally, "when you love what you do, you can hang on for dear life through all the risks and kicks and falls, and it's worth every bump, every bruise. But when you stop lovin' it, when you keep on doin' it for all the wrong reasons, well sir, that's when it becomes dangerous. It's like it turns into a coiled rattler, ready to strike, and you start circlin' it, avoidin' it, afraid of its bite. It scares you. And it scares you so bad, you start to hate it. Know what I mean?"

I shook my head.

Tony nudged me from his chair, pushing an extra toward me with his boot. "Let me tell you a tale."

I edged toward the door. "Um, I really should be going—"

"It's me or class. Take your pick."

I picked—and perched on the edge of the seat.

Tony's leather chair squeaked as he settled in, hands crossed against his stomach, gaze fixed on mine, eyebrows prickling with intensity.

"Back when I was not much older than you are now," he began, "back before the invention of cactus"—I couldn't help but smile, and Tony winked—"well sir, I didn't like myself much then. Oh, it's not important why. It was a long time ago. But what I did like was ridin'. The wilder the horse, the better. I was good at it too. That surprised everyone, I think. They didn't expect much of me when I first joined the circuit. I was just a kid to them. A no-name nobody."

He chuckled. "But then I started winnin'. The crowds used to go wild hearin' my name announced over the loud speaker. *TO-ny!* they'd cheer. *TO-ny Ma-ca-RO-ni!* I loved that. Made me feel like I was Somebody after all."

He glanced at the photo again. A smile stroked across his lips, like the tail of a horse, flicking at a fly.

"But then the more I won, the more I *needed* to win. And that's when I started to worry. What if I couldn't hold on as long as last time? What if the crowds started cheerin' someone else? What if all my winnin' was a fluke? And the biggest 'What if' of all: What if I wasn't as good as everybody thought?

"Well sir, that's when ridin' became dangerous. I started fearin' it, avoidin' it, droppin' out of competitions. People thought I'd lost my nerve. Thought I was afraid of getting hurt—or killed. That wasn't it. I was afraid they'd all find out what I'd always known deep inside: that I stunk. So, I quit. One day, I hung up my hat and spurs, and walked away. End of story. You can breathe now, son."

I let out a thin whistle of air. I'd started to feel like that meatloaf mummy from last night. Trapped. Wrapped tight.

I held on to the question I wanted to ask next. Held on to it because I was afraid the answer would cinch my chest even tighter . . .

Tony replaced the photo in its tucked-away spot on

his desk. His brows relaxed and wiggled. "Don't look so sad, son. Nowadays, I get all the, uh, *kicks* I need from bein' a school nurse. Pun, of course, intended." He glanced at the wall clock and slapped his hands against his knees. "Sixth period already! We both have work to do. Here's your pack, Sneeze. Go on now. *Git.*"

TWELVE

CLASS WAS NOT an option. I'd used all eighteen "ways" from The List during periods one through five, and had nothing left for math or PE. Rather than face those teachers empty-handed, I hid out in the boys' restroom during the next two classes, scribbling new ideas on The List for tomorrow.

At last the end-of-school-bell rang. I jammed the notes into my pack and rushed out to the bus. I was met on board by an ovation so standing, it almost knocked me over.

"Bravo! Encore!" Pierre cried, flinging his beret into the air.

"Author! Author!" yelled Goldie. She snagged my arm and pulled me to the farthest seat, where she sat to get the OSV (Optimal Snooping View). As I stumbled down the aisle, kids reached out to pat me, pluck at my shirt, shake my hand, laughing and shouting:

"Way to go, Sneeze!"

"Inspired, Sneeze!"

"She deserved it, man. She's finally met her match!"

"Whatcha got up your sleeve for tomorrow, Sneeze? We can't wait!"

Even Ace, lounging in the second to the last seat, gave me a thumbs-up.

"What's going on, Goldie," I demanded, after Pierre grabbed me by the shoulders and with ceremonial solemness planted a kiss on each of my cheeks.

"*You're* what's going on!" she said with a crow of glee.

"What are you talking about?"

Goldie grinned. "Your showdown with Fierce, of course!"

"My show—?"

The bus lurched forward with a belch and a roar, flinging us onto the rear bench. My pack slammed to the floor. Goldie seized it, saying: "Oh, you should've seen her when you left! Everyone kept clapping and laughing after your hula, and she just stood there, frozen. I'm talking solid. Absolutely *iceberg*!"

Pierre nodded. "She was totally freaked out. Then, when zee office lady call on zee intercom and tell her she eez sending you back, Miz Pierce turn white as baking flour, and look ready to collapse like a fallen soufflé!"

"Wow," I breathed. "It *did* work."

"What worked, Sneeze?" Goldie asked with a sly, knowing smile.

"Nothing, nothing," I muttered.

Pierre was on a roll. "Then Ace get into zee act! It was magnifique!"

Ace shrug-bowed. "It was the least I could do for Hiccup."

"What did you do?" I asked.

Pierre laughed through his nose. "Ace gets up to

91

sharpen not one, not two, but *three* pencils while Miz Pierce eez trying to talk. Then zee whole class eez lining up to sharpen zee pencils, and Miz Pierce eez frothing at zee mouth like a cappuccino machine. Finally she meet her Waterloo, so she make us put zee heads down on zee desks!"

"It was *great,*" said a kid from our class. "We got to sit like that for the rest of the period. Didn't have to work or anything!"

Ace yawned. "I took a refreshing nap."

"AH-HA!" Goldie exclaimed. She had unzipped my pack and held The List in her sneaky hands.

"Hey, give me that!" I lunged toward her.

She scooted toward the window, clutching The List to her chest. "I *knew* you were up to something! This is it! You're writing another book! *101 Ways to Bug Your Teacher.*"

She closed her eyes in bliss. "Oh, Sneeze, why didn't you tell me? We are going to make so much money! There are probably four times as many kids at Jefferson than there were at our elementary school. Can I please be your District Manager in charge of Special Orders and Purchasing, just like last time? Oh, please, please, pretty please?!"

I snatched The List from her hands. She had such a stranglehold that one huge corner ripped.

"What are you doing?" she hollered. "That's valuable property!"

"No, it's *private* property." I shoved The List into my pack and sat on it. Everyone hung out of their seats staring at me, their faces expectant, ears practically growing like Pinocchio's nose to hear what I had to say. "Go on about your lives," I instructed them. Then, lowering my voice, I said through gritted teeth: "There's no book, Goldie. No sales, Goldie. No District Manager in charge of *anything*, Goldie."

The sly smile returned. She tapped sparkly fingernails against her chin. "So you're not writing a book. Then what *are* you writing, and why?"

I gulped. Squirmed atop my bulgy pack. Avoided her eyes by staring at a trampled page from last week's school newspaper, the *Jeffersonian Times*, that had stuck to the bottom of my shoe.

Goldie followed my gaze—and gasped.

"Were you—were you planning to submit The List to the *Times*?"

"Huh?"

"You know, like an article or something?"

"Oh, yeah." I said. "That's it, Goldie. How'd you guess? Boy, I can never pull anything over on you. But hey, I've changed my mind. This isn't for public consumption, so let's just drop it, okay?"

"No, it's *not* okay!" She whipped out her notebook. "I can see it now: not a one-shot article, but a weekly column written by you, each one listing ten new ways to bug our least favorite teachers!"

Pierre and several other kids nodded.

"Our readership would explode," Goldie rambled on, scribbling in her notebook. "And The List would be such sweet revenge against Fierce, against all the mean teachers at the school! Of course, to keep Mr. Garrett from censoring the paper, we'd have to title your column something like: '101 Things Kids Have Accidentally Done That Bugged Their Teachers.' That sounds innocent, right?"

Pierre coughed delicately.

"Right," I said, with a mental coughing of my own. "Mr. Garrett would *never* catch on to that one."

"So you'll do it?" Goldie asked. "You'll write the column?"

The bus idled at the first stop. No one got off. Almost every face within range turned toward me. I could almost hear the kids holding their breath, waiting for my answer.

Have to admit, for one brief, insane millisecond, I was tempted. I mean, if I was looking for the optimal way to get into trouble, labeled "immature," and kept out of Patrick Henry High . . .

But I couldn't do it. I didn't want other kids using The List to bug cool teachers like Mrs. Kasai or Mrs. Tibbits. I didn't even want them bugging *uncool* teachers like Fierce. This wasn't about revenge. It was about me and only me. That's how it had to stay. I'd finish what I'd set out to do, then destroy The List.

"Not interested," I said to Goldie. "Thanks, but no thanks."

I heard grumbles and groans. Several kids stomped down the aisle, shooting me dirty backward looks.

The bus shuddered forward again.

Goldie tossed her mane. "You *can't* keep a gold mine like this to yourself. You owe it to your fellow students. *You owe it to Hiccup.*"

"She eez *good*," Pierre murmured to Ace.

"What do you mean?" I asked.

"Fierce treated him like a worm yesterday. She treats all of us like that. Number ten on the Death Roll should read: *Wriggle on your belly in the mud*!"

I didn't answer. I happened to agree 100 percent. But inciting students to turn every class into coleslaw wasn't going to help my friend—or any of us. It would only make things worse.

"I gotta go," I answered, and jerked to my feet. "This is my stop." We were a block from Gadabout Golf.

Trying not to trip, I picked my way over the packs and feet and icy silence that now filled the aisle. At the bottom of the stairs stood Hayley, arms crossed, her cold blue eyes chilling me even more than the silence.

"Don't bother getting off the bus," she said, her voice colder than her eyes. "You're fired."

THIRTEEN

"I–I'M WHAT?" I stammered.

"You heard me," Hayley replied. *"You are fired."* She snapped an about-face and marched down the street toward Gadabout.

"Hayley, wait!" I waved the bus to go on, and started after her. "Hayley, you *can't* fire me!"

She snorted. "I just did."

"I mean you can't fire me like *that.* Not without telling me *why."*

She snorted again. "I just *did."*

I finally caught up to her. "But we're *friends."*

She didn't look at me. She kept marching, staring straight ahead. "Friends don't tell friends lies."

"Lies . . . ?"

"I was on the bus. I overheard your conversation with Goldie."

"All of it? Did you hear all of it? If you did, then you'd know–"

She interrupted with a slash of her hand. "I heard enough. You told me you're not writing a sequel. You are. You told me you'd meet me for lunch with an explanation. You didn't. You told me that Gadabout is important to you. It's"—her voice sounded strained and thick, like she had a sore throat—"not."

"It *is.*"

"Huh." She stopped and SOS-ed down her nose at me. I felt small. Shrunken.

"School used to be important to you too, Steve," she said. "Now look at how you're acting. Everyone's talking about what you did in Ms. Pierce's class. It's rude and it's wrong and I . . ." She swallowed. "I don't think I can be friends with someone who thinks it's funny or fun to be a hoodlum."

I thought of Hiccup. Of Mrs. Kasai and Mrs. Tibbits, and . . .

"I don't think it's funny or fun either," I whispered.

"Tell me another." She set off, head high, her white-blond hair a smooth cap, unruffled in the breeze of her march.

Now *I* had the sore throat. It burned cold and hard, like I'd gulped a frozen milk shake. I coughed and tears pricked my eyes. I scrubbed at them with a fist.

"Oh, yeah?" I said. "Well, you're just mad because I won't tell you the *real* reason I'm making The List. If you knew, *then* you'd understand. If you were a true friend, you wouldn't have to know why. You'd *trust* me."

She didn't flinch. She kept walking.

Toward Gadabout.

Away from me.

I was losing them both and she didn't care . . .

Hayley skimmed through the squeaky, rusty gate of the golf course, shutting it in my face with a metallic clang that vibrated deep in my chest.

I gripped the bars. "Fine!" I shouted. "See how long this place holds together without me! There's only so much you can do with duct tape and a stapler!"

I spun on my heel to cross the graveled parking lot. I got four steps away.

Six steps.

Ten . . .

"Steve!" Hayley called, her voice urgent. *"Wait!"*

A scrap of hope snagged on my heart. "What?" I answered, turning.

She thrust a hand through the bars. "Keys, please," she demanded coolly.

I stood frozen, gaping at her outstretched hand.

She wanted the keys.

My keys.

My keys to Gadabout.

I tugged them from my pack and dangled them before me in the sun. They clink-tinked like a tired old wind chime in a halfhearted breeze.

"Okay," I said.

"Okay," I said.

"*OKAY,* be that way!" I thrust them into her palm. "Take your stupid keys on their stupid chain! This place is just a rotting, run-down, ramshackle–"

A gasp of air gushed from Hayley's mouth, the way it had the time she fell off her bike, belly flopping into the dirt. Then she whirled–and was gone.

***

Half an hour later, I stood on the front steps of the

Denardo house. I had to see Hiccup. Not just to make sure he was better. Not just to apologize for making him freak out. But to make sure he was still my friend. I mean, at the rate I was going this afternoon . . .

Mrs. Denardo answered my knock. She wore a grubby sweat suit and one faded bunny slipper. In her arms she held Comet, their hyperactive wiener dog.

"Oh, thank goodness it's you," she said, averting her face to avoid Comet's lightning-like tongue that was aiming to lick her chin. "The washer's been on the fritz for days. We've got a mountain of laundry. Come on in."

"Actually, I came to see Hector," I said, shutting the door behind me.

"He's upstairs, resting. I'll send him down. You know where the utility room is." She scuffed around a hockey stick and a pair of Rollerblades lying in the middle of the floor, and nearly tripped over Vixen, their chocolate Lab, who was dozing on a dog bed, nursing yet another litter of puppies. "Hec-*tor*!" she yelled up the stairs. "Stephen is here! *Horatio,* didn't I ask you three times to put your hockey stuff away? *Humph*-rey, get down here now and give this dog a bath!"

"Which dog?" a bored voice shouted.

"I don't care! Any of them! All of them! Just do it *now*!"

I dodged a couple more canines and made my way into the utility room. "Mountain of laundry" was an understatement. More like a spewing volcano.

I hunkered in front of the washer, using my headlamp to peer inside. Dasher and Dancer nudged me, oozing we-desperately-need-a-bath odors. They stared, panting

99

and drooling, at the washer's porthole window. D & D think any appliance with a window is an oven, and therefore will soon emit meat.

"*Huuuck!*"

I turned to find Hiccup, swaying like he'd just stepped off a half-hour ride on the Corkscrew roller coaster.

"Hic, are you okay?" I asked. "Tony told me you went to the doctor."

"Truth," he answered. "My physician prescribed bed rest and a sedative to help me relax and *huuck!* ease the frequency and severity of my spasms."

I noticed he wasn't hicking as much as he had the last two days. His hiccups were slow, thick, like an air bubble pushing up through a vat of molasses.

"Did you tell your mom or the doctor what happened?"

"Of course I *huuuck! huuuck!* did not! I did not wish to ruin the Plan."

So he *was* still my friend.

I shoved the washer away from the wall, ducking behind it so I wouldn't have to see his trusting, cock-eyed expression. (The sedatives had kicked in.)

"About the Plan," I began. "This afternoon, in Fierce's class, when you—when I–"

I heard a soft thud. I peeked over the edge of the washer and saw that my friend had slid between D & D, using their bodies to prop himself up.

"There is no need to say another word," he said. "I understand that the Plan could be jeopardized if you relate more than I *huck!* need to know."

"But you looked . . . and your hiccups sounded . . . I mean, I think you should know exactly what I'm doing so that what happened to you today doesn't happen again. Because what you saw in Fierce's class is just the beginning."

"In that case," Hic muttered, his eyes doing a strange polka, "until the Plan has been successfully completed, I simply *will not* return to world history."

"You can't do that!" I said. "Attendance is mandatory in Fierce's class! If you don't work with us on the Egyptian project, you'll get an F. Remember when you flunked PE in third grade? You broke out in hives the size of pizzas!"

"Pizza . . . yes, do not worry, Mom. I will not forget to tip the pizza man."

"What? Hic, wake up. We're talking an *F* in world history, remember?"

He blinked. "Oh. Yes. Well, in the event I fall short of a gassing parade, *huck!* a passing grade, I will repeat the class next year. Perhaps you will allow me to use your mummified chicken idea for my history project."

I was honored. Humbled. "So, um, you think the chicken was a good idea?"

"Not was," he answered. *"Is."*

I jerked my wrench to loosen a stubborn, sticky bolt. The wrench shot out of my hand and clattered across the linoleum.

"What else is disturbing you?" Hiccup asked.

"Hayley fired me. I–I don't think we're friends anymore. Don't ask why. I can't tell you because . . . of the Plan."

Hiccup looked as if he was trying to bristle with indignation, but all that happened was that one eyelash fluttered.

"But she has long been your comrade! Your confidante! Your *huck!huck!* plum! I mean *chum*."

"Ex-plum, now," I said with another wrench of the wrench.

He gave a long drowsy blink. "So how will you . . ." He yawned. " . . . acquire the money for the Prevention Contention?"

I felt that frozen milk shake burning in my throat again. I hadn't even thought about the money. I'd only thought about . . .

I shook my head. I didn't want to think about what I'd thought about. When I did, I couldn't remember how to breathe.

But what about the money? I *had* to think about that. Even with Mom and Dad matching my earnings, if there weren't any earnings to match . . .

"The club!" I shouted.

Startled, Hiccup jumped. He'd dozed off. "Wh–what tub?" he asked.

"*Club,* Hiccup. With all that happened this afternoon, I completely forgot about it! Remember I said I joined a club at lunch? Well, it's an inventor's club. And there's this contest. With a two-thousand-dollar first prize! I'm going to enter the Nice Alarm, I'm going to win, and *that's* how I'll get to the convention."

Winning was more vital now than ever. Once my inventing skills had come back full force, everything else would fall into place. I could explain to Hayley why I'd been acting like such a hoodlum. We'd be friends again. I'd have my job back again . . .

"Thas goob," Hiccup murmured. "You will need to exsqueeze me now *huck!,* Sneezle. Sedative . . . making me soporific." He keeled over, snoring, using Dancer's body as a pillow.

"Hiccup?" I jostled his shoulder.

"*Zzzzzz–huck!–zzzzzz.*"

He looked so peaceful, so relaxed at last, I didn't have the heart to wake him. Instead, I covered him and Dancer with a dirty towel plucked from the top of the laundry volcano, finished fixing the washer, then let myself out the back door.

FOURTEEN

THE NEXT TWO days surged ahead like a perpetual motion machine. I'd started the Plan with the pedal to the metal, and there was no idling or turning back.

The List grew. And grew . . .

I deserved an Olympic gold medal in distance for the spit wads I lobbed. I could erect a skyscraper with the late slips I earned. I lost count of the times I got sent into the hall when answering "How much should I pay?" to a teacher's request of "Pay attention, please."

"Is everything all right at home, Steve?" Mrs. Kasai asked.

"Is something bothering you, Señor Wyatt?" asked Mr. Gomez. "We could talk together for a few minutes after class, hombre to hombre."

"Perhaps, dear," Mrs. Tibbits quavered, her fingers touching my forehead in a palsy of worry, "it would be best, dear, if you saw the nurse?"

"Yes, thank you," I said.

"No, thank you," I said.

"I feel fine," said I.

I couldn't meet their eyes, though, when I answered. I didn't want to take the chance that they'd see right through me and bring the Plan to a screeching halt.

So instead, I revved it higher. And higher . . .

There were highlights:

The Wall of Froggy Fame I created in biology, using five packs of chewed bubble gum to display thirty dissected frogs on Mrs. Kasai's bulletin board.

Mr. Hunter's face, splitting into a facsimile of a painting from Picasso's cubist period, when he caught me doodling on my desk.

Miss Aguilar dismissing our entire algebra class a half hour early after I'd asked thirty times in thirty minutes: "Is this going to be on the test?"

And in Fierce's class . . .

Whew. What a relief Hiccup hadn't been present for *those* performances. If he hadn't already been ordered to bed with what his doc called Intractable Hiccups (meaning, they hadn't stopped yet), my antics and their effects would've sent him there for sure.

Eight Death Rolls in two days. That had to be a record. My Grammy Award–winning moment, though, came when I rolled Hic's famous number four: *Sing three verses of "Old MacDonald Had a Farm."*

I'm not the greatest of singers. So, instead, I performed the song with my underarm, using the key of, uh, burps. When six other guys joined me in an armpit a cappella, the class erupted into hysterical chaos. Fierce nearly toppled off The Tower in her haste to send us into the hall.

"You," she'd said, following me, her teeth gritted, her voice a roiling boil. "Detention. My class. Tomorrow. After school."

"Let me check my schedule, okay?" I asked, pulling out

my day planner. "Yes, I think I can squeeze you in. Would three o'clock be suitable?"

I caught a glimpse, just a shiver, of what looked once more like . . . fear. Then her usual explosive expression returned, and she slammed the door in my face. I was left alone to wonder why she hadn't sent me to the office again, what in the world it would take to get me sent to the office again . . . left alone to wish there was some way to get me there sooner rather than later.

As the old saying goes, you really should be careful what you wish for.

***

Wednesday and Thursday were lonely. Hayley still wasn't speaking to me, and Hiccup was still at home, sedated, under doctor's orders. Maybe I'd loan him the Nice Alarm over the weekend. Its nice manners might cheer him up; the precise, friendly ticking might soothe him. That thought lifted my spirits as I hurried to the Friday meeting of the Inventor's Club.

"This must be the Polite Alarm," said the Amys.

"No, it's the Courteous Alarm," the Amys said.

"You're both wrong," I told them, revolving my invention on a lazy Susan I'd brought from home so they could admire the alarm from all sides. "It's called the *Nice* Alarm because it wakes you up *nicely*. No annoying buzzers or obnoxious clanging. When it's time to get up, this gloved arm lowers and taps you on the shoulder. Here, allow me to demonstrate."

The Amys closed in.

"Ooooo," said the Amys.

"Ahhhhh," the Amys said.

I could feel my face grow warm, like when you're peering into a toaster, waiting for the bread to pop out. I'd spent the last two afternoons and evenings holed up in my room, fine-tuning and polishing my masterpiece (when I wasn't working on The List, that is). It took my mind off the fact that I wasn't at Gadabout with Hayley, or at Hiccup's bedside, helping him to write his latest installment of Medicine Man. Mom never noticed I was tinkering, not studying. She'd worked late every night at the lab to catch up on the experiments she started before getting the flu.

"So this is IT, the famous Nice Alarm," July Smith said, sailing into the room. She plunked a stack of clipboards and books onto the table, then swung the lazy Susan this way and that, her forehead furrowed in concentration. The alarm stared blindly back, a large, boxy toad, *tick-ticking* merrily on parade.

"Sort of primitive, isn't it," she pronounced, "but that will be easy to fix, a little paint, a little glitter, and we can use chenille, instead of this gardening glove you've got stuck on the arm now." She scratched notes as fast as she talked; short, sharp strokes on a clipboard with a black marker. "We need a different clock face too, something cuter, something less squatty. Amy, as soon as Sneeze pays his ten-dollar dues, you and Amy can go to the craft store to buy what we need. It shouldn't take us long to whip this into shape." She glanced at her watch. "Gotta run, Clubbies. Three more meetings to hit this hour. All in favor of making the final changes on our entry at the next meeting say 'aye.'"

"Aye," said the Amys.

"Aye," the Amys said.

"All opposed?" July headed for the door.

"That would be me," I called after her.

She froze. Stared over her shoulder. Lifted an eyebrow. "*Excuse* me?"

"I like the alarm the way it is," I answered. "I'm not making any changes."

July turned and bestowed on me the lips-only smile. "Well, we certainly can't enter the competition with *that*, we'd be laughed out of the exhibition hall. If we're going to win—and I have every intention of winning—then this invention has to be Perfect with a capital *P*."

"Perfect," agreed the Amys, nodding.

"With a capital *P*," the Amys agreed.

I glared at them. "You two were pretty 'Impressed with a capital *I*' up until a minute ago. And what's all this 'we' stuff? This is *my* invention. I'm not changing one single screw nut."

"Didn't you read the fine print?" July asked. She riffled through a stack of papers attached to one of her clipboards, whisking out the familiar yellow-neon flier. "'Open to all Middle School and Junior High School Inventors' Clubs,'" she read aloud. "Not individual students. *Clubs. One entry per club.* A club must have a minimum of *four* members."

"It's *my* invention." I scooped up the alarm, clutching it close. "I don't want anybody else's names on it. I'm the one who built it. *Re*built it."

I thought back on the months I'd spent on the alarm:

making pages of careful notes and drawings in my invention journal . . . hammering, bolting, pinning, gluing . . . experimenting with model after model, some that wouldn't keep time, some that spit up springs, and one that whapped instead of tapped, karate-chopping Hiccup so hard, it almost amputated his nose. Strange, but during all those long days and late nights of work, I'd never once felt tired. Not half as tired as I did right this minute.

I clutched the alarm even closer. "I'm sorry," I said. "No offense or anything, but I can't put your names on this. It's *mine*."

I'd heard that when some people get angry, their faces actually turn purple. I'd never seen it happen–till now.

The Amys took a step backward, eyeing July like she was a rabid dog.

"Hey, it's okay," the Amys soothed. "Sneeze can come up with another invention idea just like *that*."

"Yeah," the Amys echoed. "Like *that*."

My chest squeezed tight. Tighter.

"I've got it! How about a homework machine!" the Amys said.

"Yeah, a machine that does your homework!" the Amys agreed.

"You already have one of those," I said. "It's called your brain."

The Amys exchanged confused glances.

July weaved her long hair into a French braid, jerking the thick strands into place, glaring at me from under her dark brows. With each sharp tug, I winced.

We three waited. And waited.

July snapped a rubber band around the spiky ends of her braid. By then the purple had faded from her face. She glided forward, swirling me in her sweet aroma of vanilla.

"Sneeze," she murmured, fingering the collar of my shirt. "I have a confession to make. This is embarrassing, but I already submitted the entry forms to the convention committee with all four of us listed as builders of the Nice Alarm."

"You *what*?!"

"I'm *so* sorry," she said. "I thought you understood the rules, and I *had* to submit the entry, today was the deadline." She rubbed the edge of my collar between two fingertips, then smoothed a wrinkle and plucked something off my sleeve. "Don't be mad, Sneeze, we need you, you have to help us, we can win this thing with the Nice Alarm, I know we can. Just think how that win will look on our records, good high schools and colleges just eat up that kind of stuff."

"I–I don't want to think about high school," I answered. July's aroma was starting to tickle my nose. It was sweet. Too sweet.

"Then think *prize money*," July said. "Two thousand dollars, Sneeze! That's five hundred apiece. Isn't there something you'd like to buy with five hundred dollars?"

I scrubbed at my itchy, tingly nose. There was only one thing and one thing only that I wanted to buy: a trip to the national Invention Convention®.

Was it worth the price? Was it worth putting July's and the Amys' names on the Nice Alarm?

"We need you, Sneeze," July repeated. "You have to help us. You *have* to."

"Okay, sure," I said. "All right."

The Amys let out a sigh so loud, it sounded like air rushing from a balloon.

"But when the convention is over," I continued, "the alarm belongs to me again. Only me. Agreed?"

July's cool fingers met mine in a delicate handshake. "Agreed," she said, and bestowed me with the bright smile that never reached her eyes. "Bring the alarm to the next meeting, and we'll get to work."

FIFTEEN

AS I STOOD in line to buy a sawdust burger, I noticed a trio of eighth-grade girls huddled nearby. They peeked at me over the top of the latest edition of the *Times*, nudged each other, giggled, then went back to reading.

I checked to make sure my fly wasn't open. Or that I wasn't dragging a tail of toilet paper from the bottom of my shoe. Or both.

Neither. Must've been my imagination. Or maybe they were staring at the Nice Alarm. Its arm poked from the top of my pack, like I'd stuffed an elf in there and he was waving for help.

I shoved the alarm deeper. On my way to the picnic tables, I noticed that more and more kids had their heads buried in the newspaper until I trotted by. Then they nudged or nodded. Winked. Pointed. And whispered.

One girl gave me a thumbs-up. A guy mouthed *Way to go!* Another kid asked for my autograph. Before I could ask why, he smiled and murmured, "Your secret is safe with me."

Even Hayley looked me in the eye, something she hadn't done in days. When I caught her glance across the quad, I noticed she'd lost that chin-tipped angry expression she'd carried since Tuesday. Instead, she shook her head in a sad, disappointed way and shoved the *Times* into the nearest trash can.

What was going on?

"You sly dog!" Goldie yelped, plopping down on the bench next to me. "You had it planned all along, didn't you?"

"What are you barking about?" I asked.

"As if you did not know!" Pierre said with a grin. He slid onto the bench across from us; Ace stretched out next to him on his back.

"No, I *don't* know," I insisted. "Did you write something about me in your column, Goldie? Because if you did, I swear I'll–"

She squealed. "Oh, what an exclusive for *Goldie's Gossip*! An interview with Mr. Anon E. Mouse, himself! We'll do it after the columns stir up more curiosity and chaos. Maybe by then you'll even reveal what 'FH' stands for."

"Eff Aich?" I said. "And who is Mr. Nonny Mouse?"

"Why, *you* are!" She thrust the *Times* into my face. "Didn't you know you made the front page?"

I gaped, unblinking, unbelieving, at the headline:

101 THINGS STUDENTS DO THAT
BUG THEIR TEACHERS
The First in a Series of Columns
by Mr. Anon E. Mouse
(FH)

"I didn't write this," I said.

Ace peered over the edge of the table, arched a brow, and lay down again.

Pierre tsk-tsked. "False modesty eez *so* unbecoming!"

"I didn't write this," I said louder, thrusting the *Times* back into Goldie's hands.

"Of course you didn't," she said with a wink. "You should've told me you wanted to remain anonymous. Not that it'll do any good. I mean, *everyone* knows you wrote *101 Ways to Bug Your Parents*. And with the way you've been acting in class, it doesn't take a brainiac to figure who's the author of this."

Now I understood. I had a track record, so everyone assumed I was Anon E. Mouse! Which meant it was only a matter of time before the staff assumed it too. Then they'd know the truth: that this whole week had been a performance, that Sneeze Wyatt wasn't really an immature, obnoxious punk, but a smart schemer with a motive.

Worse, they'd think my motive was a publicity stunt for the article.

"But hey," Goldie was saying, "if you want to remain the Mystery Man, that's okay by me. A good journalist never reveals her sources."

"You're not listening, Goldie," I said even louder. "I didn't write the column. None of these ways were on *my* List. They're good ideas. Some of them are—whoa!—potent. I wish I *had* thought of them. *But I didn't.*"

Pierre laughed. "If you did not write zee list, then I am not French!"

"You're *not* French," I replied. "You're from Oklahoma. And your real name is Peter, remember?"

114

Pierre leaped to his feet, his chest thrust out like a rooster's. "I have been insulted! I challenge you to zee duel!"

"Gonna stab him with a soup ladle?" Ace murmured from beneath the table.

I ignored them both. "Goldie, where did the *Times* get this list?"

"My editor found it in our Suggestion Box, where *you* slipped it yesterday morning while playing Stealth Postman."

"Goldie, don't you see? Anyone could have submitted this list! Think about all the kids who overheard us talking on the bus the other day. Someone stole my idea, and is using it for his or *her* own evil purposes."

"Well, it certainly wasn't *me*." Goldie flicked a finger with disgust at the article. "I would *never* have been lame-o enough to give this up for free. Not after all the moola we brought in last year with *101 Ways to Bug Your Parents*."

The end-of-lunch bell rang.

Goldie rummaged through her pack for her recorder. "Ooo, I've got to get Fierce's class on tape! Now that the whole school has The List, I wonder *who* will try *what* in her class. You're gonna have stiff competition, Sneeze. Not that it matters. Fierce is already losing her touch. Everyone's noticed. I mean, you've taken the sting out of the Death Roll. Kids aren't embarrassed by it anymore. Now it's *cool*. And that's made Fierce almost—what's the word Hiccup uses?—anorexic!"

"I think you mean apoplectic," I said.

"Whatever." She stood, gathered her things, and promenaded across the quad, Pierre at her elbow. They disappeared within the crowds of kids who were chattering, cajoling, and jostling toward fifth period.

Only Ace and I lagged behind. He shrugged at me as if to ask *Are you coming?*

Instead I said: *"I didn't write that column."*

He stared deep into my eyes, then shrugged again. "I believe you."

"You *do*?" Wow. Ace, the Coolest of the Cool, Mr. Never-Take-Sides, believed *me*. With him on my team, maybe I could get him to—

"Don't quote me," he added, and sauntered toward class.

I followed with all the zip of a sloth slogging through tar.

Now that the whole school has The List, I wonder who will try what in her class. . . .

Goldie was wrong, I thought as I slogged. The question was: Who would try what in *which* class? Every teacher at Jefferson was at risk. The Plan was at risk. Not only would havoc reign, but I'd be seen as just one of the many wreaking that havoc.

I couldn't go to class. I couldn't go on with the Plan. The jig was up. Ruined. Obliterated.

I nibbled a thumbnail. I needed time to regroup, to think . . .

Maybe I could hide out in Tony's office again. Pretend I'd caught Mom's flu.

No, Tony would only call Mom to take me home, and I didn't want her to miss more work.

116

Besides, Tony might want another campfire chat. He'd recognize the bulge of the Nice Alarm in my pack and start asking about my inventions again.

"Hey, Sneeze, great article!" a girl shouted from across the hall.

"Yeah, great," agreed a jock, poking me in the ribs as I passed. "Got any ideas for *101 Ways to Bug Your Sister*?"

A clot formed around me. More kids. More voices.

"How about *101 Ways to Bug Your Sister AND Your Little Brother*!"

"I live with my grandparents, Sneeze. Got a list of ways to bug them?"

"I need *101 Ways to Bug Your Neighbor's Dog*. His barking keeps me awake all night."

"I'd give you five bucks for a list like that. No, make it ten!"

"Just don't go over to the Dark Side, Sneeze. My parents already know 101 ways to bug *me*!"

I elbowed forward and finally broke through the clot. "Um, yeah. Thanks for your suggestions," I said, sidling away. "They're all great. I'll keep them in mind."

"I wouldn't recommend that, Mr. Wyatt," warned a simmering voice.

I turned and glanced up—or, rather, *down*—to find Fierce waiting (for me?) at the door of her class. When not perched atop The Tower, she stood barely as tall as a fourth grader. A *short* fourth grader. I'd never been so close to her before. I could see a salting of pale freckles across her nose, a fringe of soft dark reddish lashes hemming her green eyes, a copy of the *Times* in her hand.

I gulped.

"So," she continued, "the reasoning behind your behavior this past week becomes crystal clear. It was all a preview of coming attractions." She tapped the paper against her palm. "Well, let me assure you, Mr. Wyatt, the show is over. The curtain must come down. Otherwise, you risk losing certain privileges. Very special privileges."

I wanted to dance. I wanted to cheer. She was going to keep me out of Patrick Henry High! The jig wasn't up, after all. The Plan had worked!

"Is that a threat or a promise?" I shot at her.

She seemed to edge backward, a slight shift from toes to heels. Then she leaned toward me again. "Neither. It will be a *consequence* of your actions, Mr. Wyatt. Try any of these"—she waved the *Times* in my face—"in my class, or any other class at this school again, and you'll find yourself staying here—"

"*Yes?*" I coaxed.

"—while the rest of your little club attends the Invention Convention.®"

SIXTEEN

MY EYES WERE full of green. The sizzling green of Fierce's eyes as she stared into mine. The green felt like acid, the meaning of her words burning into my brain and sizzle-seeping straight to my toes.

"I think we understand each other, don't we," Fierce said at last.

I nodded. At least I think I nodded. It could've only been a blink. But I understood. She wasn't keeping me out of Patrick Henry High, after all. She wasn't even sending me to the principal's office. She was fighting fire with fire.

"Good," she said, and returned at a clip to the class-room, her high heels popping against the floor like sparks from a fire, her hot-red hair fanning across her back like an impenetrable heat shield.

I staggered behind her. Bumped a hip against a desk. Stumbled on a chair. Thunked into my seat. Ignored the blur of nods and low-fives and thumbs-up from the bod-ies around me; faces smiling with expectancy, giggling with anticipation, lips read-whispering The List in the *Times,* wondering: *Which one will he try first?*

Goldie eased out her tape recorder and with a grin, switched it on.

Fierce perched atop The Tower, arms crossed against her ever-buttoned blazer. She crossed her legs too, her whole body tight as a fist.

"This is my class," she announced. "*My class.* I'm in charge here. Not you. I. You will treat me with respect. You will treat history with respect. *This*"—she held high her copy of the *Times,* pointing to the bugging article— "*will not be tolerated.*"

She crinkled the page into a wad and tossed it in the trash.

"To ensure that," she continued, "you will no longer have the privilege of working together in here. Your Egyptian groups will work after school, on your own time, not mine. In here, you will give me your full attention, and do as I say. You will work quietly. You will speak only when spoken to. You will not leave your seat without permission. Anyone who steps out of line before the History Faire will automatically *fail this class.*"

A pall of surprised, indignant voices rose into the air, spreading like smoke over us as Fierce's words sunk in.

"But what if I've gotten all A's on my tests this semester?"

"My parents will kill me if I flunk this class!"

"We can't speak *at all*? What if we have a question?"

"AND . . ." Fierce went on, as if she hadn't heard, "I will see to it that you repeat this class, next fall, *with me.*"

Silence.

Goldie peered at me from behind a hunk of hair, and mouthed *Do something!*

Pierre caught my glance and wriggled his nose in a

wrinkly dance I translated to mean: *Well?! What eez it you are waiting for?!*

Other kids peeked at me. Eyes wide. Waiting. Wondering. *Pleading.*

I stared at my desk, tracing a penciled sphinx doodled in the corner.

How did Fierce know about the Invention Convention® and the club?

"That's better," she said, her tone smug. "Now, take out your history books. Read chapters thirteen and fourteen, and answer the essay questions." She slid from The Tower and with a last eye-flash, began grading papers.

No one moved. No one said a word.

Then, backpack zippers unzipped. Books were pulled out with only a whisper of nylon. Pages riffled. Pencils scritched across paper.

A folded note appeared at my elbow. I recognized Goldie's loopy, frilly script. Hunching over so no one could see, I opened it.

We began a fast and furtive communiqué, sneaking peeks at Fierce to make sure she didn't notice:

> *Aren't you going to do something?*
>
> No.
>
> *Don't you have something up your sleeve?*
>
> No.
>
> *But you've got all those great ideas on The List! Try one. Any one.*
>
> No.
>
> *If you do it now, everyone will follow your lead and we can bring Fierce to her knees!*

No.

You've got to! You owe us!

NO.

Okay, I was saving this for an emergency, but things don't get any more emergent than this. I know something you don't know. Something IMPORTANT. I'm prepared to tell all, but if I do, you need to take care of Fierce and take care of her NOW. Here goes. Here's the dirt. You'd better sit down. Wait, you already are sitting down. Ha-ha! YOUR MOM IS PREGNANT.

"*WHAT?!*" I shouted.

The entire class jumped.

Fierce's head jerked up. Her gaze crackled, scanned the class, seeking the culprit. She eyed me. She stood. Her mouth opened—

The tone on the intercom pinged twice. "Excuse the interruption." The school secretary's soft voice echoed from the speaker above Fierce's head. "Would you send Stephen Wyatt to Mr. Garrett's office, please?"

The class gave a gasp of pity.

"Right now?" Fierce's eyes never left my face.

"Immediately, please."

The intercom pinged off.

Amazingly, Fierce was *not* overjoyed. Instead, her gaze kind of shivered, like she couldn't bear to see me. She glanced away, like she was almost afraid. It was the third time this week I thought I had seen that look.

Why would Fierce be afraid of *me*?

The shiver was gone in an instant. Only the green

remained. The sizzling, acid green. Then Fierce spoke one word. It seethed. It scalded.

"Go," she said.

I went.

***

"Sit down, Mr. Wyatt," Mr. Garrett instructed, pointing to one of two puffy leather chairs facing his desk.

I sat in the closest one and sunk straight to the bottom. The thick cushions oozed up around me, trapping me like quicksand. I gulped.

My mother is pregnant!?

No, don't think about that. You're finally in the principal's office.

There hung his diplomas . . . there sat his well-thumbed books and school annuals . . . perched next to a framed photo of a smiling lady and a pimply kid in a graduation gown, was his phone . . . he would use it to call Patrick Henry High, saying: *I'm sorry, but we've decided to keep Stephen Wyatt with us next year . . .*

I would twitch my lips, as if trying not to cry. I would stammer and stutter, and pretend to pretend to be brave. Then I would say:

My mother is pregnant!?!?

No, no. That's *not* what I would say. Mentally, I pushed the words into the depths of the quicksand chair.

I understand, it's quite all right, I would respond to Mr. Garrett, putting him at ease. Whoa. Wait. Wrong. That would be the *mature* thing to do. I had to continue my immature act a bit longer. Scowl and rest my chin on my chest. Kick sullenly at the carpet. Maybe belch. Then he'd

123

know he'd made the correct decision. The logical decision.

My mother is pregnant!?!?!?

Mr. Garrett rolled the sleeves of his crisp white shirt up to the elbows, as if about to perform surgery. Then he studied several papers spread across his desk, all the while thumbing his bristly mustache.

"Mr. Wyatt," he began at last, "as you know, your parents are hopeful that you can be promoted to high school in the fall. Because of that, I and your teachers have been keeping tabs on you lately: monitoring your coursework and grades, checking on your extracurricular activities, such as the Inventor's Club–"

Ah, so that's how Fierce knew . . .

"–and I must say I am distressed to have received so many"–Mr. Garrett paused, thumb poised in midair–"*comments* about your behavior the last few days." He resumed stroking his mustache as if it were a pet caterpillar. "We all care about your success here at Jefferson. And frankly, we're concerned that you seem to be headed into trouble."

My mother is pregnant?!?!?!?!

"So far this week," Mr. Garrett went on, "you've been rude, crude, and generally disruptive in almost every class. I know that you know this behavior is unacceptable. In fact, this behavior is totally unlike you. You've always been a relatively model student. So is something going on at home, or here at school, that is troubling you?"

My mother is pregnant?!?!?!?!?!

"Are you sure there isn't something I can help you with? Something you'd care to discuss with me or your guidance counselor?"

124

My mother is pregnant?!?!?!?!?!?!

"No? Well, I'm glad to hear there isn't a problem—at least, not on your end. But I'm left with a big one. Perhaps you'd care to explain this." From beneath the pile of papers, Mr. Garrett pulled out the front page of the *Times,* Anon E. Mouse's column circled in bright red.

Someone rapped on the door.

"Ah," Mr. Garrett said, rising, "that would be your father. Come in!"

Dad hustled in, his hair and sweater in their usual rumpled appearance.

"MY MOTHER IS PREGNANT?!?!?!?!?!?!" I shouted.

Dad froze. His hair and clothes too seemed to freeze in suspended animation. "How did you find out?" He glared at Mr. Garrett. "Did *you* tell him? Wait, how could *you* have known?"

"I—"

"Goldie told me, Dad," I interrupted. "Is it true?"

Dad shook his head. "Goldie? How did she . . . ? Wait—her mother." He began muttering to himself. "Barbara ran into her at the doctor's, but surely she wouldn't have . . ."

"I gather," said Mr. Garrett, motioning for us to sit down, "that there *has* been something going on at home that's troubling you, Stephen. It's only natural when there's a new addition to the family for you to feel—"

"He didn't know," Dad said, interrupting.

"Daaa-aaaad, is it—"

"True?" Dad finished. He ran a hand through his tangled hair. "Yes."

125

"B-but—" I sputtered. "You never! You couldn't! You didn't! We didn't—"

"Perhaps, Stephen," Mr. Garrett soothed, "it'd be best if you waited outside while I talk to your father for a few moments." He ushered me into the main office. "Just a few moments," he repeated, gently closing the door in my face.

I stood and stared at the plaque on his door. *James Garrett, Principal.* The name blurred, like when you spoon-mush the letter-noodles in alphabet soup.

I couldn't believe it. Mom and Dad had done it again. Dropped another Atom Bomb on my life. Only this time was worse. Far worse. This time, there hadn't even been a warning. This time, I hadn't even gotten a fish.

SEVENTEEN

"WHY ARE WE stopping here?" I asked Dad as he eased his Cad into a narrow parking space at The Scoop, the local ice cream shop. We hadn't said one word to each other since leaving the school twenty minutes before. I'd been "excused" by Mr. Garrett for the rest of the day.

"I'd like to talk without your mom overhearing," Dad answered. "And there's nothing like some Rocky Road to help us along a rocky road." He gave a thin smile, unbuckled his seat belt, and swung open the door. "Chocolate or vanilla?"

"I'm not hungry."

"I swear, no ketchup or salsa."

"Chocolate, then. With chocolate sauce. And chocolate sprinkles."

Dad shuddered. "Where *do* you get your bizarre eating habits?"

I closed my eyes and leaned back against the candy-apple red seat. I heard the door's metallic slam, and Dad's footsteps receding up the walkway.

The sun beat hot on my head. I could imagine Hiccup fussing over me, a slop of sunscreen in his hand, saying:

Apply this to all exposed areas of your body. You do not want to incur precancerous keratotic lesions . . .

I missed Hiccup. I wanted to talk to him, tell him about Mom and my visit to Mr. Garrett's office. Tell him about Anon E. Mouse's column, and how Fierce had found out about the Inventor's Club and the convention and was blackmailing me into being the Perfect Student. Well, at least now that I was forced into my best behavior, Hiccup could come back to class.

If his hiccups had stopped . . .

"Here you go." Dad reappeared, holding my cone wrapped in a wad of napkins. He plunked into his seat and bit into a rounded mound of ice cream the color of an army uniform. "Avocado," he mumbled through the bite. "Flavor of the Day. Closest I could find to salsa."

I licked at a few chocolate rivulets melting onto my hand.

"Yes, it's true," Dad announced, as if our conversation in Mr. Garrett's office had never been interrupted. "Your mom is going to have a baby in about eight months."

I glared at him, my words hot as the sun on my head. "And just *when* were you going to tell me, Dad? When Mom was packing to go to the hospital? When the kid was graduating from college?" My words flowed hotter, faster. I hurled my uneaten ice cream cone into a nearby trash can with a fierceness that rattled even me. "What else have you failed to mention? Whoa, maybe it's not just a baby. Maybe it's twins! Triplets! Hey, who knows? Maybe they're not really my siblings, after all. Maybe I'm adopted! Left on your doorstep twelve years ago by alien pod people!"

128

Dad choked and his cone snapped in half. With a fist-ful of napkins he mopped at the cone-crumbles, smearing the greenish blobs of ice cream across his pants.

"I know you're angry, Steve," he said, taking a last glance at his lap and raising his hands in an I-give-up ges-ture. "Especially learning the news from *Goldie,* of all peo-ple. Oh, that mother of hers! The next time I see her, I–well, never mind. What matters is, we *were* going to tell you. We only found out yesterday, and your mom wanted a few days to get used to the idea."

"Oh," I mumbled, sliding low my seat. "Sorry."

"It's all right." He ran a hand through his rumpled hair, adding a streak of avocado. "We're all a little stunned. Especially your mom. She's forty, you know. Not exactly *old,* but there can be risks when a woman that age is preg-nant. She's scheduled in two weeks for a test called an amniocentesis. It's done in the hospital, takes about an hour. The results will let us know if the baby is growing normally, if everything is all right."

"But everything *isn't* all right!" My stomach clenched. "Mom's been so sick this week, she practically pitched a tent in the bathroom!"

Dad chuckled. "Oh, that's just morning sickness. No big deal. Don't tell your mother I said that. She's miser-able. But it's normal for women to feel queasy and exhausted in the beginning. Happened when she was pregnant with you too. Goes away after a while."

I could feel my stomach muscles uncoil a bit, until I remembered–

"But, Dad, can you and Mom afford to have another

kid? You guys work such long hours now. Did you set aside some money for this?"

Dad's cheeks flushed pink. "Uh, we didn't exactly plan this baby, Steve."

"You mean it was an accident?"

"We-ell . . ." He waved his sticky hands in a vague circle. "I don't much care for that word. I prefer to think of it more as a . . . surprise."

Some surprise. I mean, when you hear that word, you think of parties and presents . . . *not* dirty diapers.

"Wait. One. Minute," I said. "I'm not going to have to change its diapers, am I? And where's it going to sleep? In *my* room? With *my* inventions? And where are you going to get the money for those diapers and teddy bears and rattles and stuff? Are you going to dip into my Invention Convention® fund?"

Dad touched my knee. His voice too was a touch, like a friendly, reassuring arm across my shoulder. "Steve, your money stays your money. That's a promise. Yes, you'll have to share your room. Can't be helped. That's one reason why it'll be so great to attend Patrick Henry. You'll be able to do all your inventing, keep all your inventions safe, at school."

My stomach resumed its boa-constrictor-like squeeze.

Did this mean that Mr. Garrett *wasn't* keeping me at Jefferson next year, even after calling Dad into his office?

I slumped farther into my seat.

Dad started the engine and swung the Cad out of the parking space.

"And speaking of school–" His voice was stern now.

130

Accusing. "Mr. Garrett didn't exactly call this afternoon to offer me the job of PTA president. So what's been going on this week?"

"Nothing," I grumbled.

"Don't give me that. It was Something, all right. An unacceptable Something. You've been disrupting your classes. Frustrating your teachers. They can't do their jobs when you act like that. You can't *learn* when you act like that. He's willing to give you another chance, Steve. To still consider transferring you to Patrick Henry. But you'll have to stop this so-called 'research' for your next book or these articles you're writing."

"I'm not writing a book!" I blurted. "I didn't write the article in the paper!"

"Then what's this about?"

"Nothing." I crossed my arms. "And I don't want to talk about it."

"I see." He nosed the Cad into traffic and sped up. The rush of wind lifted my hair, cooled the sweat on my scalp and face.

Dad raised his voice over the wind. "You're grounded this weekend for Nothing, then," he said. "And I expect this Nothing at school to stop at once. Your mother is nervous and scared and nauseous enough as it is without having to pile worry about you on top of it all. So *cut it out*. Or you won't be going to the convention this summer, even if you *do* earn the money for it in time. Do you understand?"

I nodded. There was nothing else to do, to say. . .

We arrived home ten minutes later. Dad maneuvered

the Cad into the garage like he was docking a large boat, and switched off the engine. "The diapers aren't so bad, Steve," he said, with a strange, faraway smile. "Actually, changing a baby's diaper can be an especially bonding experience."

"Bonding?" I said, aghast. "What do babies poop . . . superglue?"

He laughed. "Diapering can be a quiet, tender time for both of you, where you have his full attention. You can talk and sing and blow raspberries on his tummy. That used to make you giggle like crazy!"

"Huh," I said, sounding like Hayley.

"You have to realize, Steve, that this baby will be your little sister. Or brother. He'll look up to you, admire you, want to grow up to be *just like you.*"

Fat chance of that, I thought. What was there to look up to? I was a has-been inventor. A has-been friend. A has-been plotter, schemer, dreamer. I should accept the fact right here and now that I'd be a has-been brother as well.

EIGHTEEN

"YOUR MOM'S HOME early," Dad commented, noticing Mom's car. "She must not be feeling well again. Mum's the word about our 'visit' to the principal's office, understand? She doesn't need to know, and I don't want her upset. She's gotten ultra-emotional on top of everything else."

"Okay, okay," I mumbled, brushing past him, grabbing the cordless phone off the kitchen counter. I headed for my bedroom, punching numbers as I went.

"And not one word to Hiccup about the baby," Dad called after me as if reading my mind. "Nor anyone, till your mom is ready to announce the news. But *especially* Hiccup. You know how he feels about her."

An image flashed through my mind: Hiccup zip-hicking here at warp speed to fan Mom with palm fronds and hand-feed her grapes. Seedless grapes. *Peeled.*

I punched the Off button.

"How who feels about whom?" Mom asked, appearing at the top of the stairs. Her hair and T-shirt were sleep-mussed, but she smiled over the banister at me.

I gaped at her stomach. Couldn't help it. My eyes were yanked to The Spot like it was a super-powerful magnet.

Yet, there was nothing to see. Her stomach wasn't sticking out like she had a watermelon under there. Not even a grapefruit.

"Uh, hi, Mom," I said, my voice sounding scratchy. "Dad told me about . . ." My eyes yanked to her stomach again. "You know."

"About the baby?" Tears glazed her eyes. "Isn't it wonderful?" She rushed down the stairs, clasped me in a hug, and snuffled into my ear. I patted her back, wondering if I should offer to move some heavy furniture for her.

"It's cool, Mom," I said, trying to mean it but still feeling . . . how *did* I feel?

"I hope it's a girl," Mom whispered. "It'd be nice to have a baby sister, wouldn't it? Although another boy would be wonderful too."

Dad hurried out of the kitchen, a package of ground beef in his hands. "How about barbecued hamburgers for dinner?" he boomed.

She eyed the green stains on his pants and gasped. "You ate *ice cream!*" More tears glazed her eyes. She stumbled into Dad's arms now, muffling her words into his shirt. "I've had *such* a craving for a banana split. With pineapple, and whipped cream, and chocolate sauce . . . "

"There, there," Dad said, ushering her into the kitchen. "We could pour chocolate fudge on a scoop of cottage cheese . . . "

Mom wailed.

I took the opportunity to hide out in my room and click Redial. Even if I couldn't tell Hic about the baby, it would be good to hear his voice.

Or, rather, his hicking. He was still at it. Nonstop. His fourth straight day.

"Does the doctor know what's causing this?" I asked. "Can you eat? Can you sleep? When can you come back to school?"

"No. *Hic!*" Hiccup answered. "No. *Hic!* No. *Hic!* He doesn't know. *Hic!*" I heard him take a drink, and that seemed to help. "The tranquilizers have not been effective. If these spasms do not ease soon, my physician will admit me to the hospital ASAP for a CT, MRI, EKG, and—"

I gulped. "Surgery? You're going to have *surgery?*"

"No, no. Just a few tests to make sure nothing physical is causing me to *hic!* If the results are negative, we can assume my problem is merely stress-related."

"Hiccup, that's one reason I called," I said. "I have stress-reducing news."

I began to explain how the Plan had failed, that I wouldn't be bugging my teachers anymore, so it was safe for him to come back to school. But dodging each hic was like trying to race through a torrential hailstorm without getting nailed. Mentioning Fierce's name had caused his hics to hail harder, faster.

Then I heard a high, irritated voice, a scuffle, and his mom came on the line.

"Sneeze? What on *earth* did you say to him?! We're supposed to keep him calm, quiet. Doctor's orders. Hold on a sec . . . Ho-*ra*-tio! Didn't I ask you *three* times to stop feeding the dog peanut butter? He just threw up in Harlan's sock drawer! I don't care *which* dog! *Any* dog!

135

Hart-ley, puh-leeze take Dasher and Dancer out for their walk. They're practically digging an escape tunnel under the front door. And don't forget to open them a can of dog food. No, peanut butter does *not* count as their dinner . . . Sneeze? Listen, don't call again. Just let Hector rest. We'll let you know when he's better."

My face flushed hot with guilt. "I could walk the dogs for him tomorrow," I offered. Then, remembering I was grounded, added: "I mean on Monday. Or *any* day next week. *Every* day next week!"

The phone went dead.

Mrs. Denardo had hung up on me!

With a sigh, I clicked off the receiver. No matter what Mrs. Denardo said, I'd head over to Hic's house first thing after school on Monday. I had to do something to help my best friend. I just didn't yet know what . . .

***

I spent the rest of the weekend in my room, sneezing, blowing my nose, and doing research online for our Egyptian project. I found a lot of stuff about what the ancient queens and pharaohs ate and even what they were entombed with for an after-death snack. But there was little information about how the foods were actually prepared. I hoped that wouldn't be a problem for Chef Pierre. I hadn't exactly seen packaged ox chops or leg of antelope at the grocery store lately. The group would be meeting at my house again Friday afternoon. Pierre had promised to show us his final menu then. We'd just have to trust that roast ox would be tastier than Dad's ketchup burger.

Now and then, as I worked, I'd gaze at the Nice Alarm

and bask in its brisk *tick*. I tried to imagine it all doozied up, the way July wanted it for the convention: a dainty, sequined glove, patent-leather doll shoes instead of foot pads, fluttery false eyelashes on its face. The image made me want to barf peanut butter in Harlan's sock drawer. I couldn't believe I was going to let her do those things to *my* incredible creation.

Yet, what choice did I have? Going to the convention was more critical than ever. It was my only hope of smashing my inventor's block to smithereens.

Besides, the Queen of the Clubs and the Amys were counting on me . . .

***

Sunday night, late, the phone rang. The jangle rocketed me out of sleep. Heart hammering, brain soggy as milk-logged cornflakes, I bolted upright and fumbled in the dark for the receiver on the nightstand.

"I *told* you she was preggers!" came Goldie's gloating, goopy voice.

I peeled open one eye to read the Nice Alarm. "Goldie," I groaned. "It's eleven forty-seven. *At night.* Shouldn't you be, oh, I don't know, *sleeping*?"

"Naw. Not for another hour or two. I've always been nocuous."

"I'll agree with that," I muttered. "But I think you mean *nocturnal*."

"Whatever. Now listen up, Sneeze. You really need to get your next column in *before* Wednesday. That's our deadline, and besides, I was thinking it'd be cool to have Hiccup draw a few cartoons for it."

I collapsed onto my pillow. "Goldie, for the last time, *I did not write that column.* And Hiccup's in no condition to—"

She heaved an exasperated sigh. "You *don't* have to keep up the charade. We *all* know it was you. Why else would Garrett have called you into his office? So fess up and let us give credit where credit is due! You'll be a king at Jefferson. Say, maybe we could mummify a few chickens in your honor!"

"Good night, Goldie."

"At least tell me what FH stands for! You owe me that!"

"Good-*bye,* Goldie." I stabbed the Off button.

Two seconds later, the phone jangled again.

I stabbed On.

"Go *away,* Goldie!" I threatened through gritted teeth.

"Steve?"

My heart froze.

My hope froze.

My mouth formed the name in shocked surprise: *"Hayley?"*

"Yeah." It was more a breath than a word.

"Hayley."

"Yeah."

"Hayley." I could keep this up forever.

"Yeah." Maybe so could she.

"Steve," she repeated, her voice sounding faraway-ish. "It's late, isn't it? I—I'm sorry to bother you."

"It's no bother!" I sat up again and switched on my desk light, as if that would help me to hear better over the simmering of my aquarium.

"I don't know who else to talk to, and even though I know you don't ever want to speak to me again, I—"

"Hayley!"

"Steve, I need your help."

Whoa. Twice in one week. This was Serious.

"Anything," I said. "What's wrong?"

She sighed. An angry, echoey sigh. "Daddy's invited the Girlfriend for dinner. Friday night."

"Oh, no," I said.

"He says it's time I met her. Huh. Daddy and I were doing fine, just the two of us. Why did *she* have to come along? Two's company, three's a crowd."

"But when your mom was alive, three wasn't a crowd."

"That was different."

"Yeah, I know . . ."

"She's trying to take Mom's place, Steve. I won't let her. She'll never replace Mom. NEVER."

I sat up straighter, gearing myself for the challenge I knew was coming. "What can I do?"

"Come to dinner. Please. Friday night. Five-thirty. I know you don't want to. I know you're mad at me for firing you. And I'm still mad at you for—well, but—"

"I'll come," I said. "My history group's meeting here after school, but I'll be there as soon as we're done."

"Wait, there's more," Hayley warned. "During the evening, I want you to help me act out some of the 'ways.' You know, from *101 Ways to Bug Your Parents.*"

I dug a finger into my ear. Maybe there was a glob of wax stuck in the canal, mistranslating what she'd said.

"Steve? Are you there?"

"Yeah, I'm here. I don't get it, Hayley. After all the things you said to me the other day when you saw me bugging Mrs. Tibbits—"

"I *know,* but I'm desperate. I could do a bunch of stuff from your book on my own, but she might just think it's all accidental 'cuz I'm nervous. But if we're *both* doing your list, if we *both* hit Daisy with all we've got, then she'll think twice about being a stepmom to a kid who's friends with a—"

"Hoodlum?" I finished for her, my chest smarting.

The breath-sigh. "Yeah. You said yourself that's what you are."

I closed my eyes. Rubbed at my chest.

"Okay," I said. "I'll do it."

"You will?" Her voice caught. "Thanks. Thanks a lot. And if you want your old job back—"

I shook my head, even though I knew she couldn't see me. "Naw. That's okay, Hayley."

Her next words were insistent. "But you shouldn't do this for free! You do enough stuff for free, always fixing people's phones and beepers, helping them with their homework. It isn't right."

"Hey, don't worry," I said. "I'm getting paid for helping you. Honest."

"Huh."

A pause.

"I gotta go," she said. "If Daddy wakes up and finds me out of bed, he'll call the Marines. I've got to hurry back up to the house."

Back up to the house?

140

"Hayley, where *are* you?" I asked, picturing her outside in a public phone booth somewhere. In the dark. Alone.

"I'm in my secret spot, where I used to go with Mom. It's safe. Close to home. No one knows it's here. See you Friday."

She hung up.

I lay down again, burying myself in the thick, warm comforter, listening to the dial tone that moments ago had been Hayley's voice.

Funny how she didn't understand that I *was* getting paid. Way more than I'd ever earn at Gadabout. Way more than I'd ever earn on the Nice Alarm. Just her talking to me again was like making a million dollars. In solid gold.

NINETEEN

"DID YOU WANT to see me?" I asked Tony the following Friday from the door of the nurse's office.

"Come on in, Sneeze," he drawled from where he sat at his desk. He beckoned me into the room.

I stayed rooted in the doorway, holding the call notice I'd received during sixth period. "I feel fine," I said. "I've been sneezing more lately, but I think if the doctor adjusts the dosage of my meds, I'll—"

"I didn't call you in to talk about your allergies. Set a spell," he insisted.

I perched on the edge of a cot, my pack still slung over my shoulder, ready to bolt as soon as I could. "What *did* you want to talk about?"

Tony slouched into his favorite position, legs stretched out on his desk, arms crossed behind his head.

"Haven't seen you in over a week," he began. "Ten days, that's a fact. I was curious, is all. Wantin' to make sure you're okay. People have been tellin' tales."

My back went rigid. "What kind of tales? I've been a model student all week."

It was true. I'd kept my promise to Dad not to do anything to upset Mom.

Monday through Friday. Five whole days. I'd sat quietly, politely, in every single class, despite kids begging me to work my bugging magic until I wanted to scream: *Leave me alone!*

I'd been such a model student that on Wednesday, Mrs. Tibbits patted my cheek with her hand and gave me a stale macaroon.

On Thursday, Mrs. Kasai welcomed me to class with a cheerful: "It's nice to have you 'back,' Benson."

Even Mr. Garrett smiled and nodded at me this morning in the hall.

And, every single day, as I left her class, Fierce had smiled at me. A smug smile. An I've-got-the-goods-on-you-buddy-so-we-know-who's-the-boss-now-don't-we? smile.

"I haven't done *anything* wrong," I said.

"Never said you did." Tony's chair squeaked as he leaned forward. "But I heard talk in the teachers' lounge last week. Talk 'bout you not seemin' yourself. I know Hiccup's still at home, hickin' like a buckin' bronc, and the doctors are scratchin' their heads. That's gotta be hard on you, his best friend."

"Hic will be fine," I said. "Just *fine.*"

But he *wasn't* fine. I'd hurried to his house every day after school this week, under the pretense to walk Dasher and Dancer. They practically did backflips, they were so overjoyed to see me, slobbering on my hands, snuffling my pockets for meat. (Right. Like I always carry a spare T-bone.) Mrs. Denardo did *not* react with the same enthusiasm. "I thought I made myself clear, Stephen," she'd announced yesterday through a slit in the door before shut-

143

ting it in my face. "We appreciate your help with the dogs, but you may *not* see Hector. He needs to remain quiet. No excitement allowed. He'll call you when he's better."

Before leaving, I tossed a handful of pebbles against Hic's window. A freckled hand appeared through the curtains, and gave a quick wave. That was all.

" . . . there's the stress of the History Faire next week," Tony was saying. "I know Ms. Pierce is kickin' her spurs hard, gettin' y'all ready. Because of her, our school's won first place the last nine years. The pressure's on to make it an even dime. And you've entered the Nice Alarm in the Invention Convention®! I'm a mite put out you didn't tell me 'bout that. I'd like to saddle up, see what you've been workin' on."

"How do you know all this?" I demanded. "Are you *spying* on me?"

No way did I want Tony to see the alarm. It'd been hard enough for *me* . . .

The Inventor's Club had met at noon that day. When the Amys and July had finished doozying up my invention, it wasn't mine anymore. Just a skeleton of me. A skeleton of my thoughts, my hard work. The rest was all gaudy doodads and sparkly sequins, a cartoon of itself, a freak in a carnival.

"Don't you have anything better to do than peer into my private life?" I spat the words out at Tony. I leaped to my feet. "You're the school nurse. You're supposed to take temperatures and wash cuts. Well, I don't have a fever, and I don't need a Band-Aid. So can I go now?"

I expected Tony to order me out of his office. But his

face stayed calm, almost curious, his next words low and slow. "You might not be sick," he replied, "but you've got one blazin' fire in that belly. And I can tell you right now, it ain't from eatin' the cafeteria chili."

"What are you talking about?"

"You're angry, Sneeze. Good and mad. About ready to blow."

My mouth dropped open. I sank onto the cot.

"So what?" I said, though the snap had left my words. "What's wrong with being mad now and then?"

"Nuthin' at all." Tony leaned back again, balancing his chair on two legs. "It's a good sign. A healthy sign. That's a fact."

I shrugged my pack to the floor. "What do you mean?"

"Sometimes," Tony said, gazing at the framed photo of himself on the bull, "sometimes when we're feelin' lost and sad, what it really means is, we're angry. Angry like a pawin', stampin', snortin' bull. But instead of lettin' that bull out of the paddock, lettin' him run his course, we open the wrong gate. We let him charge full speed right back at ourselves. We don't know we're doin' it. We can't see it happenin'. But it happens just the same."

He gazed at the picture for a long moment, as if giving me privacy, time to let his words soak in.

"So," he went on at last, "the fact that you're startin' to get mad instead of feelin' down on yourself, is a good sign. It means you're takin' the bull by the horns. It means you're wakin' up."

I found I'd been holding my breath. "Waking up to what?" I managed to croak.

His chili brown eyes held my gaze now. "Only you know the answer to that."

I grabbed my pack. Struggled to my feet. "I gotta go."

Tony nodded and wrote out a hall pass. As I took it, he held tight to one corner with his strong callused fingers. "Come on back now, hear?"

"Sure," I said.

He released the pass, and I hurried to the door—then stopped. I remembered the last time I'd scurried out of his office, tail between my legs. There'd been a question I'd wanted to ask, a question I'd been too scared to ask . . .

"Uh, Tony?" I said, my hand still on the doorknob. "There's something else."

"Shoot."

I took a sip of breath. "It's about your riding. You were good. Really good. You loved it. So how could you stop? How could you make yourself quit?"

"Oh, I still ride, Sneeze," he confessed in a gentle voice. "I ride all the time. I only stopped ridin' for the crowds, ridin' for the prizes, ridin' for the crowds who expected me to win prizes. Ridin' for everyone except myself. Now I ride for one reason and one reason only: for the joy of it. Do you get what I'm sayin'?"

"Yeah," I said, though I wasn't sure I did. Wasn't sure I wanted to.

"Thanks," I added, and scooted out the door.

***

"Another explosive column!" Goldie announced that afternoon when the history group met at my house. She kicked off her shoes and flopped onto my bed, yanking a

146

copy of the *Times* from her pack. "Prime real estate again, Sneeze! Front and center. And The List is dynamite. I'm talking TNT."

Pierre snickered. "*Oui!* How you say in English? Ka-*boom!*"

"Let me see that!" I snatched the paper from Goldie's hands. I'd forgotten to pick up the latest issue at lunch.

Oh, not again. There IT was. Page one. Lead story:

101 THINGS STUDENTS DO THAT
BUG THEIR TEACHERS
The Second in a Series of Columns
by Mr. Anon E. Mouse
(FH)

I leaned my hot forehead against the cool glass of the bubbling aquarium. Edison, Bell, and the Wright Brothers wiggled over to offer their condolences.

Oh, man. If Dad found out about this . . . If Mr. Garrett still believed I was behind this . . . If Fierce . . .

I was doomed.

I glanced at Ace, who was lounging again in my old easy chair, reading my new untouched issue of *Invention Mania*.

"Did you see this?" I asked, waving the paper like a white flag.

He glanced up. Arched an eyebrow. "Naw," he replied. "I never read."

"I just *wish* you'd taken my advice and gotten your column to me *before* Wednesday," Goldie continued in a huff. "A couple of Hiccup's drawings would've been hot stuff with this. Where is he, anyway?"

"I don't believe this!" I hollered. "Haven't you noticed Hic hasn't been at our meetings? Haven't you noticed he hasn't been in school since the day I did the hula? Or are you deaf, dumb, *and* blind?!"

"Well, don't have a hissy fit about it." Goldie sat up, cross-legged. "You can't expect me to remember *everything* about *everyone*, you know. I've got *hundreds* of students at our school to keep track of." She gestured with her *Goldie's Gossip* notebook. "Not to mention people's, ahem, *mothers*. How is yours, by the way?" She batted her lashes with innocence.

"None of your business," I threw back at her. "But Hiccup should be. He's our friend. No, scratch that. He's *my* friend. *And* he's a member of this group. Don't you care that he's been hiccupping for more than a week? That he can't eat or sleep? And if his hiccups don't quit soon, he'll end up in the hospital?"

Ace arched two eyebrows.

"Sacré bleu!" Pierre whispered, removing his beret.

"Wow, that must be some kind of hicking record!" Goldie said. "I can see the headline now: HECTOR: THE MARATHON HICKER!" She began to scribble in her notebook.

I slammed it shut, almost grazing her nose.

"Hey!" she squealed.

"This isn't some juicy scoop for your column," I said. "This is HICCUP."

"Well, *you're* his best friend. *You're* the inventor. What are *you* doing about it?" She gestured at my invention-filled shelves. "You must have *some* plan or concoction or

148

device around here to fix him up, good as new."

"Goldie, I'm not a doctor! I'm just a kid who–"

"Excusez-moi," Pierre interrupted, waving his beret like a ref throwing in the towel at a prizefight. "I have to be home early. My mother needs me to go with her to zee"–he half gagged–"to zee health food store. So, if you pleeze, I'd like to get on with zee problem, I mean, zee meeting."

"Très smart idea, Pierre!" Goldie rubbed her hands together. "Let's see your menu for the funeral banquet."

"We-ell," Pierre went on, the word heavy with regret. "That eez zee problem. You see, there *eez* no menu."

Goldie narrowed her eyes. "What do you mean, *no menu*?"

Pierre crossed his arms. "I refuse to cook zee Egyptian meal."

Goldie's eyes narrowed further. "What do you mean, you refuse–"

"I will not do it! Zee food zees peoples ate eez unacceptable to my high standards!" Pierre threw out his chest as if the ancient Egyptians were personally insulting him, and began ticking off on his fingers: "They had no pastry! No croissants! No escargot! They ate zees coarse bread full of–oh, I can barely say it!–grit! It was so coarse, it wore down their teeth! And do you know what else? They ate boiled goat! They ate boiled ox! They ate zee same figs that zee *baboons* ate!" He shuddered and shook his head. "No. I will not waste my talents as chef on this alleged food. That eez that."

Ace shrugged, then returned to his non reading.

149

"Pierre," I urged, "get a grip. We don't have time to change topics. The History Faire is *a week from tomorrow.* If we don't have a menu, that means we don't have a project. And if we don't have a project—"

"Oh, we'll have a project, all right," Goldie said, pointing her pen at me. "I am *not* getting an F in this class and taking it again next year with Fierce. You're our chairman, so if Pierre can't cook, it's your responsibility to come up with—"

"Whoa. Wait." I had jumped to my feet, holding my hands out as a barrier. "Since when am I chairman again? I was deposed two weeks ago, remember? You ousted me. Overthrew me. Mutinied—"

"But *you're* the genius, Sneeze," Goldie said, as if that solved everything, as if the solution was so obvious even a soap dish could understand it. "You can fix this. I know you can. After all, *you're* the *inventor."*

"I AM NOT AN INVENTOR!" I hollered at the pinnacle of my lungs. Then I scooped up an armload of my invention journals from their home on my shelf, and tossed them by twos and threes out the window. *"I"*–toss–"AM"–*toss*–"NOT!"

My bedroom door opened with a loud *crack.* Mom stood there, hands on her hips, looking pale, worried—and angry. "What on earth is going on in here?" she demanded.

I faced her. My chest heaved. My breath came in gasps. "I can't pretend anymore," I yelled at her. "I'm not an inventor! I'm not! You can't make me! None of you can make me!"

I rushed past her, through the door, down the stairs, out of the house.

TWENTY

"YOU'RE LATE," HAYLEY announced in that familiar mixture of anger and wonder as she flung open the door. Then her voice softened, and I heard a ripple of worry beneath her words. "I thought maybe you changed your mind."

"Of . . . course . . . not," I reassured, in between gasps, practically doubled over to catch my breath.

"What's wrong? Your face is red. And you're *sweating*."

I nodded. "Rode . . . my bike. Fast." I had, in fact, pumped like the pistons on a steam engine. At full throttle.

"No, that's not it. You look . . ." Her ice-cream-cold blue eyes peered closer. "Well, you don't look like you. What's *wrong*?"

"Nothing . . . everything . . . nothing." How could I explain to her what had happened at the meeting if I couldn't even explain it to myself? I'd never felt like that before, never acted like that before. I'd screamed at my mom—one of the three special people in my life who needed to stay as de-freaked-out as possible right now. I'd run out of the house like a crazy person. Chucked my precious invention journals out the window like they were old Frisbees . . .

"Huh," Hayley said, but she stepped back for me to enter. "The Girlfriend is late too. That'll give us a few minutes to make a plan."

Hayley and her dad live in a spacious loft above an old surfboard wax factory. There are views of Gadabout—Big Ben's face, the apex of the Great Pyramid, the stone turret of King Arthur's Castle—from each of the sparkling clean, long, bare windows. A warmish May breeze swirled in. The polished hardwood floors squeaked under my sneakers. The place smelled like old coconut-scented wax and lasagna.

"Who's at the door, Peach?" Mr. Barker called from the kitchen. He scurried out, wiping his hands on a dish towel stained with tomato sauce. I knew right away tonight was ultra-important to him: He wore his "formal" Hawaiian shirt (the one with the jade green palm trees) and his black "dress" shorts. His hair was slicked with the orange-and-eucalyptus-scented goo, and it looked like he'd actually hosed off his flip-flops.

"Oh, hello, Sneeze!" he said. "I thought you were Daisy. We're so glad you could join us tonight. I can't believe I'm double-dating with my daughter." He shot her an affectionate grin.

Hayley snorted. "Sneeze isn't my date, Daddy. He's *Sneeze.*"

Mr. Barker winked at me. "Whoever he is, please offer him a soda. You'd better get dressed. Daisy will be here any moment."

"I *am* dressed, Daddy," Hayley said.

"I meant, you'd better change."

152

"I *did* change, Daddy."

He eyed her outfit: a shrunken, faded T-shirt. Jeans with holes in both knees. Hair uncombed. Hands filthy, like she'd dug dragon sludge out of Gadabout's moat.

Mr. Barker sighed. "Change again, Peach. That outfit is inappropriate." He scurried into the kitchen.

"Huh," Hayley said. "Did you notice he set the table with Mom's *good* china? And her lace tablecloth? That's the stuff Grandma gave them when they got married. It belonged to my great-grandmother. We haven't used it since Mom—"

I could see a lump as she swallowed.

The phone rang.

Hayley ignored the jangle, her mouth twisting. "It's probably the Girlfriend again," she grumbled. "She's called about forty times."

She led me into the living room, flopping down on the rug, pulling a copy of *101 Ways to Bug Your Parents* from beneath the sofa. "Let's talk strategy. I've been studying this, and I'm not sure if we should start out slow—chewing with our mouths open at dinner, slurping our food—or if we should begin with a bang."

She tapped a finger against her cheek. "How about this: When Daddy introduces us, you sneeze into your hand before you offer it to her to shake. If it's a big, gooky sneeze, we could have her out of here before dessert!"

"Sneeze, that was your mom on the phone," Mr. Barker called, poking his head out the kitchen door. "She sounded worried. Said you left the house in kind of, uh, a

153

hurry. She also said that your invention journals are still strewn all over the front lawn, and if you don't want them watered, you need to pick them up as soon as you get home before the sprinklers go on tonight."

"Great," I muttered.

"Why are your invention journals on the lawn?" Hayley SOS-ed.

I sighed. "It's a long story."

The doorbell rang.

"Oh, gawd, that's *her*." Hayley pulled a pack of bubble gum from her pocket and unwrapped all six pieces, shoving them into her mouth.

I put both my hands on her shoulders, and stared straight into her eyes. "It'll be okay," I said. "After tonight, she'll be history."

Mr. Barker rushed into the room, holding the spatula, not even noticing that Hayley hadn't changed. "This is it!" he cried. He threw open the front door.

Hayley edged away, tugging me with her. We couldn't see anything but Mr. Barker's palm-treed back.

We heard murmurings. A quick kiss. Then, Mr. Barker turned and they strolled in, arm in arm, smile in smile.

She was barely as tall as a fourth grader. (A short fourth grader.) She had a salting of pale freckles across her nose, a soft fringe of dark reddish lashes hemming her green eyes, and her blazing hair was pulled into a bouncy pony-tail.

She looked young. Friendly. Sweet, even.

I felt as if I'd been punched in the stomach.

Daisy was history, all right. *World history*.

"Hayley, Sneeze . . ." Mr. Barker began. "I'd like you to meet—"

With what felt like my last gulp of breath, I whispered: "Fierce!"

"No, not Fierce," Mr. Barker assured me with a nervous laugh. "*Pierce*. Daisy Pierce. Do you two know each other?"

In a flash, Fierce's smile froze, faded, then returned small and thin. She hesitated and glanced at Mr. Barker as if to ask: *Is this some kind of joke?*

At last she held out a hand. I stuck mine out too. It moved in a jerk. The handshake was quick, barely a touch, the way enemies shake before a duel. "Yes, of course we know each other," she said, her voice low, wary. "Steve is in my fifth-period world history class."

"If I know Sneeze, and I do," said Mr. Barker, clapping me on the shoulder like a proud dad, "I'm sure he's one of your best students."

I made an inward groan.

"He's a young man of *many talents*," Fierce agreed. "Did you know he can even dance the hula?" Her lips still held the thin half smile, but her eyes simmered full green. "I'm sure you'll be performing it for us again very soon."

"Um . . ." I said.

She turned to Hayley. Her original smile returned full force, then wavered, like she was really pleased to meet her boyfriend's daughter, but didn't want me to see that she, Fierce, had a "nice" side.

"And this is Hayley!" she said with a genuine sweetness, holding out a hand. "Your dad has talked so much about you . . . "

Hayley back-stepped, stuffing her hands into her pockets. Then she blew a huge bubble, popping it with a *crack!*

Mr. Barker frowned, but said: "We should eat. The lasagna's been in the oven so long, it's almost as hard as fruitcake. Hayley, would you light the candles, please?"

"In a minute," Hayley said in a bored drawl (which I translated to mean *in a century*), and slouched into a dining chair.

"Shall I open the wine, sweetheart?" Fierce asked Mr. Barker, holding up the bottle she'd brought. "It's a Jaffurs syrah. Delicious with lasagna. *And* fruitcake."

He gave a joyous laugh. "The corkscrew is in here . . ."

They went into the kitchen.

"Sweetheart?" Hayley spit the word dripping with venom.

"I don't believe it," I muttered, wiping sweat off my forehead. "Of all the people in the world he could be dating . . ." I plunked into the chair next to hers.

"What are you *doing?*" she demanded in a whisper. "Or, rather, *not* doing? She's been here five whole minutes, and you haven't bugged her once!"

"Didn't you see who that is?" I whispered back.

"I've got eyes, haven't I?"

"It's Fierce, Hayley. *FIERCE.*"

"I know who it is. And I don't care if she's the Queen of England! You promised you'd help me!"

"I can't, Hayley. I'm sorry. I wish I could, but I *can't.*"

156

Hayley shot me the frostiest SOS I'd ever seen. "Can't? Or *won't?*"

Okay, so I'd shouted to the world that I wasn't an inventor. I hadn't meant it, had I? I'd been an inventor once, so maybe I could be again. But I'd have to get to the Invention Convention® to find out if I still had inventing in me. If I did what Hayley asked, there was no way I'd ever know. Fierce would see to that three seconds after she left here tonight.

"Both," I admitted to Hayley. "It's not that I don't want to help you, but Fierce has got something on me. She's using it as blackmail. I can't explain now, but–"

"Here we are!" Mr. Barker swept in, placing the lasagna and a bowl of leafy salad on trivets in the middle of the table. Fierce gave Hayley and me each a root beer, then poured wine for Mr. Barker and herself.

Hayley sent me an SOW (Squint of Wrath) mingled with a pain so deep, it stabbed my heart.

"The dinner smells heavenly," Fierce said, unfolding a linen napkin.

Hayley burped.

"And the table looks just gorgeous," Fierce struggled on. "Are you the flower arranger of the family, Hayley?"

Hayley chortled with a mouthful of root beer until a stream shot out of her nose onto Fierce's plate.

Mr. Barker leaped up. "Daisy! Let me grab you a clean plate. Honestly, Peach, try to drink more slowly, all right? And spit out that gum!" He disappeared into the kitchen. Hayley spat the gummy glob onto the lacy tablecloth.

Fierce's eyebrows zoomed skyward. Then *she* shot me an SOS.

157

My toes curled. Oh, man, she thought I was responsible for Hayley's behavior! I had to do something–quick.

I cleared my throat. Used my nicest, politest, most interested voice. "Um, so how long have you been teaching, Fier–Ms. Pierce?"

"This is my fifteenth year," she replied, serving herself a wedge of lasagna on the clean plate Mr. Barker brought her.

"Daisy used to teach first grade," he announced, like it was the most fascinating thing since the invention of the wheel.

Hayley yawned. Noisily.

Daisy winced around a nibble of salad, but tried again. "Have you ever done any babysitting, Hayley? If not, you should try first graders. I love that age. They're like kittens, full of wonder and curiosity. The world is so new to them. Around every corner there's–"

"Cat pee," Hayley put in.

Fierce ignored her. "–something to pounce on! Explore! Discover! They're sweet and smart, and they love to hug."

"Ewwww," Hayley said, wrinkling her nose. "Daddy, this lasagna smells disGUSting! Can I have a peanut butter sandwich?"

Mr. Barker put his fork down with a loud clank. "No, you may not! And what's wrong with it? You made the same recipe last week!"

"Well, this week it's disgusting!"

"Hayley, sit down and eat."

"I'm not hungry! Can I have some ice cream?"

158

"No! Sit down, please!"

She sat, arms crossed, chin on her chest, a scowl on her face, and kicked me in the leg. "*Do* sssssomething!" she hissed.

"Um, would you please pass the salt?" I asked Fierce.

"That's *not* what I meant," Hayley muttered.

Mr. Barker cleared his throat. "Tell us, Daisy, why'd you switch to seventh grade?"

"It wasn't my choice," Fierce answered with a sad smile. "My husband and I divorced, and I was short on money, so I moved down here from Santa Barbara. Teaching seventh grade at Jefferson was the only position available, so I grabbed it." She took a sip of wine, then held Mr. Barker's gaze, her cheeks flushing. She seemed to have forgotten that Hayley and I were there. It was weird to see her green eyes without the acid. Weird to see her blazing hair without the flames.

"That first year was the worst, I'll admit," she went on. "Worse than worst! I'm a little on the short side, and every student towered over me like a skyscraper. I was so scared! They knew it too, and took total control of my class. I didn't know what to do, how to handle them. They were so different from first graders! It was humiliating." She shook her head. "I almost quit after that first year. But I'd always loved teaching, so I hung on." She glanced at me, as if just now remembering who—and what—I was. The softness in her voice faltered. The simmer returned. "Eventually, though, I got the hang of it," she finished.

Oh, she'd gotten the hang of it, all right. By turning the

tables with the Death Roll. Instead of them humiliating her, now she humiliated *us*.

"Fascinating!" Mr. Barker said, chin in his hand, glowing at Fierce with the admiration for someone who'd just established world peace.

Hayley stuck a finger down her throat and pretended to gag.

"Okay, that's it!" Mr. Barker threw his napkin onto the table and glared at his daughter. "I've had enough of your behavior, missy."

"*My* behavior! What about *yours?*" Hayley squinted across the table. "Mom's good china, Mom's lasagna, you're even wearing that shirt, the one Mom bought you right before she—"

Mr. Barker wasn't listening, wasn't hearing. "I don't know what's got into you tonight—"

Fierce put her hand on his arm. "Sweetheart—wait—"

"—but it's completely unacceptable! You need to apologize to Daisy. And to me and Sneeze. Then I want you to go to your room. Stay there until you can sit and eat and talk like a civilized human being!"

"Oh, I'm going, all right!" Hayley leaped to her feet, knocking over her chair. "I don't want to see you"—she pointed at her dad—"or you"—she pointed at Fierce—"and especially"—she pointed at me, took a ragged breath, tears filling her eyes—"*you* . . . ever, *ever* again!"

Then she turned, slammed out the front door, and raced down the front metal steps and out into the night.

TWENTY-ONE

MR. BARKER SAT tracing the lacy pattern of the table-cloth. I watched his finger move up and around, dip and down. I don't know what Fierce was doing, because I was too busy watching that finger. It looked sad with its nail bitten to the nub and a fleck of tomato sauce caught in the wrinkles of one joint.

No one said a word.

An ice age came and went. A frostiness lingered in the air.

"I'm sorry, Daisy," Mr. Barker murmured at last. "I don't know what's gotten into her tonight . . ."

Fierce covered his hand with hers. "I do," she replied.

I gulped. She blamed me. I knew she blamed me. At any moment she'd fix me with those hot green eyes and—

"Gosh, thanks for dinner!" I said, folding my napkin into a neat square. "The lasagna was delicious. Or would've been, if I'd ever tasted it. Bye!"

I escaped Fierce's gaze. Escaped the room. Hurtled down the stairs and out into the night.

"Hayley!" I shouted. *"Hayley!"*

She couldn't have gotten far. I had to find her. Had to explain . . .

I peered into the darkness. Saw the shadow of Gadabout's gate. It stood half open, squeaking in the breeze. I eased through it and blasted onto the course.

Two weeks since I'd last been there. It felt like two minutes. It felt like an eon. I slowed to a trot, sucking in the scent of home: the dank moat . . . old, cold corn dogs . . . plastic, peeling palm trees . . . the oily aroma of machinery. Ah, machinery. Cogs and wheels. Pulleys and gears. Gadgets and motors that spun the Windmill, raised the Drawbridge, burbled the Volcano, pumped my heart . . .

I meandered every path, peeking into every corner, calling her name.

No answer. Only a dog in the distance, barking to hear its own voice.

Hayley wasn't there.

But she *had* to be. She felt the same as I did about this goofy place. It was her home away from home. Her sanctuary. Which meant her secret hiding spot had to be here too. *I've got to hurry back up to the house,* she'd said the other night on the phone. *It's close. Safe. No one knows it's here . . .*

Yes, it had to be at Gadabout.

But where?

I retraced my steps. The dried-out AstroTurf paths crisped beneath my shoes like potato chips.

I'd worked here almost a year. I knew every nook and cranny of every hole. Knew them as well as my own bedroom: the Pirate Ship, the Windmill, the Abandoned Gold Mine, Big Ben. I'd tinkered with, repaired, or expanded every mechanism of every single one of them, except–

The Great Pyramid.

It stood before me, solid. Impenetrable. Its thick cement blocks rose high, slanted, to a mute point. No windows. No doors. Only a slot the size of a mouse hole at its base, for the golf balls to shoot through. The pyramid had no moving parts. So there was no reason to get inside of it, no reason for it to have a trapdoor.

But it did.

The partial moon grinned like a Cheshire cat. By the silver of its smile, I could just make out, along the right-hand corner, a rectangular outline.

I unhooked the flashlight from my tool kit and flicked it on.

There. To the left of the block. A tiny button, like a miniature doorbell. I pressed it. The block sprung open; a door on a well-oiled hinge.

Flashlight in my mouth, I crawled on hands and knees along a hard cement floor, through a tight and musty tunnel, following a warm, yellow glow.

The tunnel ended, opening into a stuffy room with an angled, pointed ceiling. In ancient Egypt, this would've been the sacred tomb of a pharaoh, filled with his favorite food and treasures. Instead it held plush cushions. A tattered rug. Old children's books. A teddy bear, missing one eye. Rickety table, with pens and paper. A glowing lantern.

And, sitting on one cushion, her back against the wall, knees hugged to her chest: Hayley.

She turned her head to look at me. The SOS was gone. The anger was gone. So were the tears.

"Hi," she said.

"Hi."

"You found me."

"Yeah."

"Huh." One corner of her mouth twitched with a hint of smile. "Took you long enough."

I sidled over to where she sat, and sunk down on the cushion beside her.

"So this is it—your hiding place."

"Yes."

"It's cool."

"Yes."

"Your dad doesn't know it's here?"

"Nope. Mom rigged the trapdoor herself. She was an engineer, did I ever tell you that? Well, she was." She raised her chin and gazed across the small room, as if staring into the past. "She made it when I was three. Said we needed a place for just us girls. Where we could tell secrets. *Keep* secrets."

I noticed a framed photo atop the table. I couldn't help but smile at the lady—with Hayley's rice-colored hair, her blue-marble eyes—who smiled mischievously into the camera. She held a squirming young Hayley on her lap, fingers tickling. Hayley's eyes were squeezed shut with laughter.

"She looks fun," I said.

"She was." Hayley's voice snagged. "We were really close. It hurt so much when—" She let out a long, ragged breath. "Well, you know all that. I miss her a lot, Steve. But what's weird is, I'm starting to not miss her as much. And so is Daddy . . ."

I pulled one hand off her knee and held it. It felt cold, a tight fist cupped within my fingers.

"Fierce isn't going to take your mom's place," I said. "No one will ever take her place. She was *your* mom. That won't change. No. Matter. What."

Hayley pulled her hand away, turned her face away. But I could hear the tears clotting in her throat. "Yeah. I know."

"Then what's going on?" I asked. "Are you jealous because your dad's not spending as much time with you? I mean, you guys have gotten really close. You're a team. Like Laurel and Hardy. Abbott and Costello. Tom and Jerry. *Ben* and Jerry. Oh, wait—they broke up. Now they're just an ice cream."

I was trying to make her laugh. And she did. One short chuckle. Her fists unclenched, and she wiped at her eyes with the heels of her hands.

"I'm *not* jealous," she insisted. "Huh. So maybe I was in the beginning. But I *want* Daddy to fall in love. That's the thing. It'd be great. He's been so sad the last three years. Lonely. I want him to be happy. Really, I do. And lately, since Daisy, he's been humming again. Jingling coins in his pocket. He hasn't done that since—before Mom died."

I nodded.

"But I'm scared, Steve. You're the only person I can tell. I didn't even want to tell you, because I thought you'd think . . . well, I thought you wouldn't like me anymore. The whole thing makes me sound like such a dumb baby. But I'm *scared*."

Wow. Hayley was the last person I thought could get

scared. Hayley was the last person I thought would *admit* to getting scared.

I took her hand again. This time she didn't pull away. "You're *not* dumb. You're *not* a baby. Besides, I'd be scared too if Fierce was *my* dad's girlfriend."

Hayley laughed. "I'm not scared she'll end up my wicked stepmother or anything. I'm scared that . . ." She gazed at me with a Squint of Confusion. "Steve, what if I actually end up *liking* her? She was *nice* tonight. You saw how nice she was. I acted like a total hoodlum, and she hung in there because she cares about Daddy."

"I've never seen her act anywhere close to that nice in history," I said. "She was even sorta nice to *me*."

Which was the real Daisy Fierce? I wondered. Both? Neither?

"Well, what if she keeps on being nice?" Hayley persisted. "What if it wasn't an act to get in good with me? What if she was nice because she *is* nice, and because . . . she cares about me too. I couldn't handle that. I mean, what if I end up liking her, loving her, and then something happens. What if I lose her. Like Mom . . . "

We sat for a moment in stunned silence. The silence found deep and dark inside a mummy's tomb. Centuries of quiet waiting, of waiting for an afterlife that would never come.

"Hayley, you can't think like that," I said finally. "You can't live like that. Worrying about someone dying. I mean, it could happen. I wish I could say it wouldn't, but I can't. It *could*."

My words tumbled now, like water flowing over

rocks in a river. "But you can't be like *these* guys." I motioned at the angled walls above us. "The ancient Egyptians spent their entire lives worrying about death, worrying about what would happen to them after. A hundred thousand men slaved twenty years to build the Great Pyramid. And what was that? A monument to death. Their whole culture was a monument to death. These people, they never lived in the *now*. They never lived in . . . *life*."

Again, the silence. But it had changed. I could hear Hayley's breath. Feel the warmth in her hand as she squeezed mine.

"Huh," she said after a long minute. Then she elbowed me and smiled. "You've been learning something in Daisy's class after all."

I snorted, imitating her. "Yeah, I guess I have."

"Hey, and maybe you won't get that F."

"Oh, I'll be getting an F, all right," I said. "Or worse, after tonight."

"You didn't do *anything* tonight. That's one reason I was so mad!"

"Yeah, but I'll bet Fierce thinks I put you up to all that bugging stuff," I said. "Which means I'm doomed. My inventions are doomed . . . "

"Your inventions? What are you talking about? Why are you doomed? Tell me."

"I can't."

"Why not?"

I didn't even want to tell you, she'd said, *because I thought you wouldn't like me anymore*

But I *did* still like her. So maybe–just maybe–she'd still like *me*, after . . .

I couldn't worry about the after. Not anymore. I had to concentrate on now.

I took another breath. "Hayley," I said. "I have something really important to tell you."

TWENTY-TWO

SO I TOLD her.

Even though I was scared.

Even though I was ashamed.

Even though I was angry at myself for feeling scared and ashamed.

My words inched out. It was like chipping away, piece by piece, year after year, at the Great Pyramid, until at last I stood in bright sunlight, surrounded only by a pile of rubble and dust.

I told Hayley about my inventor's block. How ashamed it made me feel. Too ashamed to tell my parents. Too ashamed to go to Patrick Henry. I explained my reason for bugging the teachers . . . for desperately needing to get to the Invention Convention® . . . for allowing the Queen of the Clubs to doozy up the Nice Alarm . . .

When I finished the telling, Hayley didn't do any of the things I thought she'd do. She didn't order me out of the pyramid—or out of her life. She didn't snort with disgust or laugh in disbelief or cringe with the shame of knowing a failure.

Instead, she leaned over and gave me a gentle kiss on the cheek.

On the cheek.

A kiss.

A gentle one.

I raised my hand to where her lips had brushed quick and light as a butterfly.

"Um," I said.

"Wow," I said.

"Thanks," I said.

We looked at each other. Then our gaze flicked away to stare at the walls. At least, I think they were the walls. Most rooms have walls, don't they? You know, those things that hold up the roof?

"What were we talking about?" asked Hayley. "Oh! I remember!" She grabbed a pencil and paper from the rickety table. "We need to make a plan."

"A *plan*?!" I laughed. "Don't you think I've made enough of a mess with the plans I've got?"

She waved a hand as if to erase all that. "We need a plan to *fix* this mess, don't you see? First, I have to apologize to Daisy. She needs to know you didn't have anything to do with how I acted tonight." She began to scribble.

"She won't believe you," I warned. "You heard what she said about her first year at Jefferson. She thinks junior high kids are hoodlums. That we're all out to get her. That *I'm* out to get her. That's why she threatened to keep me from the Invention Convention®, to make sure I'd behave in her class."

"Oh. Right." Hayley tapped the pencil against her teeth. "Then we'll just have to convince her that deep down, you're really a model student."

"I've been playing that role all week!"

"Simply sitting in class, keeping your mouth shut, and turning in your homework isn't enough. You've got to prove that you're really listening to her, *learning* from her. You've got to show her that you find Egyptian history absolutely fascinating!"

I did a Goldie eye-roll.

Hayley ignored me. "So that's number two," she said, scribbling again. "After we take care of those, we can tackle number three. That'll be hardest."

"What's number three?" I asked.

She pointed her pencil at me. "Finding out why you've got inventor's block."

I realized I was holding my breath the way I had that day in Tony's office. The day he told me he'd quit the circuit.

"I think . . ." I began, letting go of the breath, "I think I already know why I've got inventor's block. Tony and I were talking about . . . well, about something else the other day. Rodeos and riding and stuff. Except, maybe it wasn't really about something else, after all. Anyway, I think I've got this block because–"

"What?" Hayley prodded.

I took another breath. "Inventing isn't fun anymore."

There. I'd said it. As soon as I spoke the words, they became real, they became true. Because they *were* true.

"You mean," Hayley said, "inventing to you is like some awful chore?"

"Exactly."

"That's awful, Sneeze! That'd be like saying Gadabout

is a chore for me!" She shook her head, eyes closed, as if she couldn't bear that horrific thought. "So we have to change the question to: *Why* isn't inventing fun anymore?"

"I don't know. I'm not sure I want to find out. I mean, what if I can't make it fun again? Without my inventions, will there still be a . . . me?"

Hayley shot me a look. "You're going to invent again, Steve. Going to *want* to invent again. I promise. No. Matter. What."

She didn't give me time to respond. She smacked the paper and pencil onto the table, and said: "But first, I have to apologize. To Daisy *and* to Daddy. Then we'll brainstorm a way for you to dazzle Daisy's socks off." She grabbed my arm. "Come on. It's stuffy in here."

She snatched the lantern and led the way, crawling, through the dark tunnel. We stretched, glad to be out of the cramped tomb, breathing the fresh night air.

"I'm getting too big for that thing," Hayley observed, rubbing a bumped spot on her head.

"It's a cool fort," I said, "but a tight squeeze. Good thing Hiccup isn't here. He's got claustrophobia. He won't even use the stalls in the boys' bathroom. He's so chicken, he once even—"

I froze.

Solid.

As Goldie would say: absolutely iceberg.

"What?" Hayley asked. "What's wrong?"

"Chicken," I said, grinning.

"Chicken?"

"*Chicken,*" I agreed. "As in cluck-cluck. *King* Cluck."

"*What?*"

My mind spun. I don't know if it was thinking about Hiccup, or sitting in that pyramid talking Egyptian history, or if finally confessing my fears was what did it, but—

"I can see it now," I said, my arm sweeping across the star-spangled sky. "When the Great Feathered Pharaoh passed on with a feeble croak-a-doodle-doo, his beloved people suspected *fowl* play . . . "

"Steve—"

"Even the most *hard-boiled* of his flock were *shell-shocked*! He'll need a final *roosting* place. We'll have to *scramble* to get it done in time, but—"

"Get *what* done in time?"

I started to pace. I was drawing blueprints in my mind. "If the whole class works together, Group Three's sphinx can be transformed with a few feathers and a beak. Group One can change the burial masks too. We'll need a sarcophagus, of course, and a coffin for the funeral procession. In ancient times, coffins were pulled by oxen on a sled, but we could use an old wagon, hitch Dasher and Dancer to the front to—"

"Stephen J. Wyatt!" Hayley announced. "You've gone mad!"

"No, I haven't," I said. "But I *have* thought of a way to prove—for the whole class to prove—that we're not what Fierce thinks we are!"

TWENTY-THREE

FIERCE WAS GONE by the time Hayley and I climbed the stairs to the loft. The food had been put away, dishes washed, the lacy tablecloth tucked out of sight. We found Mr. Barker in his favorite recliner at the open windows overlooking Gadabout. He must've seen us coming along the path in the moonlight, but he hadn't stormed out to demand apologies or order me home. He'd just let us come to him when we were ready.

When he heard our footsteps behind him, he held out his arms. Hayley hurried over and climbed into his lap, wrapping her arms around his neck as if she were four years old. "Oof!" he said, laugh-groaning under her weight.

"Daddy, I'm sorry . . ." she began.

"I know," he answered, and stroked her hair.

I started to tiptoe backward, when Mr. Barker called: "I made you a doggie bag, Steve. If you clean your plate, you can come back tomorrow for dessert."

A laugh of relief bubbled in my throat. "Thanks, Mr. Barker," I said, grabbing the lasagna. "'Night, Hayley."

"'Night, Steve," came her shirt-muffled voice.

I clattered down the steps and hopped onto my bike to head home.

The porch light blazed above my front door, and one lamp shone in the living room, but the rest of the house was dark. Mom and Dad must've picked up my invention journals before they went to bed, because they weren't strewn across the lawn anymore. Not on their shelf, either, or on my desk or bed. No biggie. It wasn't like I needed them any time soon. While pedaling home, I'd made an important decision. A life-changing decision . . .

"You're doing WHAT?" the Queen of the Clubs screamed at me over the phone when I called her the next morning.

"I'm pulling the Nice Alarm out of the competition," I repeated. "I'm not going to the Invention Convention®."

It wasn't as hard as I'd thought it would be to say those words. I mean, if inventing wasn't fun anymore, what was the point of doing it? Of doing anything involving it?

The phone sputtered. Not the connection—July. I envisioned her face ripening into that plump-grape color. I had to hold the receiver three feet from my ear as she raged: "You CANNOT do this to me, you OWE me, we CANNOT enter this competition with only three people, without your invention. I NEED to win this—I mean, WE need to win this! The award is CRUCIAL for our permanent records, for—"

"Listen," I interrupted, peeling the glitter and sequins off the Nice Alarm. "All I'm doing is pulling my invention from the contest. You can keep my name on whatever entry you guys come up with, if you want. I don't care."

And I didn't. Well, maybe I cared a little. Otherwise, I

would've quit and let July use the alarm anyway. But I'd been a great inventor once upon a time, and I was going to go out with that greatness intact, with that self-respect intact. *With the Nice Alarm intact.* I couldn't bear to have my name on some tacky mutation of what the alarm had once been, once could've been.

"You CANNOT back out now, it's TOO late," July was saying. "What are we supposed to use as an invention, Mr. Genius?"

"You're a smart girl," I answered. "I'm sure you can concoct something." I started to tell her I was sorry, but stopped when I realized I wasn't.

"You are SO blowing this. You are in SUCH trouble. Just WAIT!" She slammed the phone down.

I hung up too, rubbing my ear. Then I finished peeling the junk off my greatest invention, and replaced it on my nightstand. I raised its arm into the "set alarm" position. We saluted each other.

Then I called Hayley.

"How'd it go with your dad last night?" I asked.

"Great. We talked a lot. Laughed too. Even Daddy, when he remembered the root beer shooting out of my nose onto Daisy's plate. I mean, he was angry, but, hey, he understands. We'll be okay. *I'll* be okay."

"I'm glad." I cleared a wad of apprehension from my throat. "And, uh, did you talk to Fierce?"

"No. I left a message on her machine, but she hasn't called back. Are you still going to mummify King Cluck?"

"I'm going to do more than mummify him," I said, looking over the notes I'd made. "I'm going to get my class to create a complete funeral for him at the History Faire. Mourners and an entombment ceremony and everything. The judges and Fierce are going to be blown away like a scarab beetle in a sandstorm! We may not win first prize, but we'll have the most original, complex, authentic project there. Then Fierce will finally understand that not all middle schoolers are hoodlums. We're not bratty kids. We're young adults—nice, responsible, *smart* young adults."

"You're the nicest and smartest of 'em all," Hayley said.

"Um, thanks."

Hayley turned businesslike again. All those years running Gadabout were good training. "So what can I do?" she asked. "How can I help?"

"Could you come over for a couple of hours? I called Goldie and told her I was ready with our 'new' project idea, and that if she doesn't want to flunk world history, she and Ace and Pierre better get their beaks here no later than two o'clock."

She chuckled. "I'll be there! Want me to pick up any supplies on the way?"

"Well, we need a chicken—"

"Dad's got one defrosting in the fridge. I'll ask him if we can, uh, borrow it. What else?"

"Let's see . . ." I riffled through my Egyptian history book. "I've already got plenty of salt and baking soda to substitute for natron—that's what the Egyptians used to dry out the dead bodies, remember? Mom's got olive oil in the kitchen. We'll rub that on King Cluck to keep him waterproof beneath bandages. We'll need spices, though. Cloves. Cinnamon. Maybe nutmeg."

"Mmmmm, sounds like we're making pie."

"In a way," I said with a cluckle. "*Chicken* pot pie!'

***

"So what's our new project?" Goldie asked with grumpy breathlessness, flouncing into one of our kitchen chairs. "I'm glad you finally came to your senses about your responsibility as chairman after that *fit* you threw last night, but honestly, did you have to *threaten* us to be here? I mean, it *is* Saturday. Some of us have *lives,* you know!"

Using a napkin, Pierre dusted off the chair next to hers before consenting to sit. "I was in zee middle of a delicate recipe, but we have arrived—how do you say—in zee nick of time!"

"Two oh one and thirty seconds," Ace observed, despite not wearing a watch or being able to see the kitchen clock from where he lounged in the third chair.

I shot a grin at Hayley, who stood, arms crossed, behind Goldie. She grinned in return with a thumbs-up.

"Here it is, gang," I announced, plunking a large tray before them, whisking the checkered cloth off King Cluck and his "accoutrements."

My seventh-grade work group leaned forward with eager eyes.

Then their foreheads wrinkled.

And their mouths dropped open.

"No," said Goldie.

"Yes," I replied.

Goldie tossed her mane. "We've been here before, Sneeze. What is this, some sort of déjà voodoo?"

"I think you mean déjà vu," Hayley corrected.

"Whatever. Either way, this is *not* a new project. It's the same old chicken!"

"On the contrary," I said, "it's a brand-new chicken, *and* a new and improved project. Now, before any of you start whining, I want to ask three critical questions. One: Do you *want* to flunk Fierce's class? Two: Do you *like* the way Fierce treats us in class? Three: If we don't mummify King Cluck here, do any of you have even a glimmer of an idea for our project?"

Goldie and Pierre shook their heads like I'd just asked them if they wanted to be exposed to bubonic plague.

Ace shrugged, but one eyebrow arched with curiosity.

"I thought not," I said. "Then listen up. This is what we're going to do."

I outlined my plan for the project. I talked for a long time. Hayley served as backup, offering suggestions and technical assistance. She had, I reminded everyone, gotten an A+ on her Egyptian project.

As I talked, Goldie's expression changed from a dismissive *you-are-out-of-your-clucking-mind* to a begrudging *this-just-might-work* to a feverish *maybe-I-can-use-this-in-my-column.*

"What a story this'll make for the *Times*," she exclaimed, clicking her pen with excitement. "Front page, with a picture of me, arm in wing, with the winning entry!" She patted the cool wrinkled skin of the featherless pharaoh; then with a grimace, wiped her hand on the tablecloth.

"Yes, but can we get zee rest of zee class to take part?" Pierre fretted. "Their projects are almost finished. And zee History Faire eez one week from today!"

"It shouldn't be a problem," I said. "Everyone hates how Fierce treats us. Everyone will benefit if she starts treating us like human beings."

"I could always inflict a bit of blackmail," Goldie offered, rubbing her hands together. "I do have *information* on everyone."

"No way," I said. "If we want Fierce to treat us with respect, then we have to be worthy of it. No blackmail. No *information*. Just lots of hard work. Are you with me? All in favor, say 'cluck'!"

"Cluck!" said Goldie.

"Cluck!" echoed Pierre.

Ace stretched. "What about Hiccup?" he drawled with feigned indifference.

My stomach clenched. "He's not coming back this semester," I admitted. "He's going into the hospital for tests, so he can't be part of our project. But his brother Horatio said we can borrow Dasher and Dancer for the fair."

"Is there anything we can do for him?" Hayley asked. "Can we send him some flowers? Can we call him?"

"He's allergic to flowers," I said, "and his mom won't let anyone talk to him. Believe me, I've tried. She just keeps saying: *He's supposed to rest. No excitement. Don't call again.* The hiccups are . . . bad."

"Poor Hic," Hayley sighed.

"Cluck," Ace murmured.

"So let's get to work," I said. "For Hiccup. For us. For all the future students in Fierce's classes!"

TWENTY-FOUR

BY THE FOLLOWING Friday, I was practically reading, writing, speaking, and dreaming Egyptian. In hieroglyphics.

Our entire history class spent every milli-moment hammering, sawing, sewing, painting, pasting, papier-mâché-ing and, uh, feathering to get the project done in time for the fair. Only a few kids had grumbled in the beginning. Mostly those in Group Three who had almost finished their replica of the sphinx when Goldie called them to propose our plan. But in the end, she turned the holdouts to won-overs. She could be very persuasive at times, our Goldie. Even without any *information*.

Besides, everyone agreed if there was even the slightest chance of changing Fierce's attitude toward us, all the hard work would be worth it.

Tempers grew brittle as potato chips, though, late Wednesday as our deadline drew near. Goldie stomped a petulant foot, refusing to wear the beak Scotty Parker designed for her *Cleopecktra* costume ("It completely covers my perky, upturned nose, which everyone says is my best feature!"); Sherry Shahan from Group One accidentally elbowed the sarcophagus, denting one wing; two guys from Group Four started dueling with paintbrushes over who would get to use the one with the mink bristles; and I kept sneezing too close to the feather bag, turning our garage into the snowflake-y aftermath of a pillow fight.

"This eez impossible!" Pierre wailed, bumping over a huge pot of glue that oozed onto our precious sheets of gold leaf. A hail of moans and curses from Group One (who were changing their burial masks to chicken heads) pelted him. He kicked at the pot. "We will never finish zees in time!"

"You just wasted five seconds telling me that!" I exclaimed, feeling like the head foreman of the great pyramid's 100,000 laborers (if they'd acted like preschoolers). "We've got to hold it together, people. We're gonna make it. Just clean up the mess and get back to work."

And work we did.

We changed King Cluck's salt and baking soda mixture twice a day to hurry along the drying-out process . . . we finished his sarcophagus, tomb, and the processional sled . . . we painted murals and masks and the display info board (Ace turned out to be an amazing artist, inking all the hieroglyphics with the elegance of a pro calligrapher— although we dared not compliment him, for fear he'd disappear in mid-glyph) . . . we created costumes for the mourners and the pharaoh's distraught queen. . . Group Four even prepared recipes for the funeral feast, including one using pig's feet. ("I will not eat it! Not one bite!" Pierre vowed with a sniff of snobbery.)

We worked feverishly on our research notebooks too, poring over historical volumes in the library and online, footnoting quotes, double- and triple-checking facts and sources, making colorful graphs and charts, and copying over every section so that each page was Perfect.

Perfection was the rule in class, as well. We did everything Fierce demanded of us the Friday before: gave her our full attention, spoke only when spoken to, didn't leave our seats without permission, never gave her cause to demand: "Death Roll!"

So, she lectured from bell to bell with a smug, satisfied smile, her green gaze eyeing us all.

All except . . . me.

Not once did she look at me. Speak to me. Or in any way acknowledge what happened at Hayley's. It was as if I wasn't in class. It was as if I didn't exist. I found that more unnerving than her famous bone-melting glare. At least when she glowered at me, I knew where I stood, knew I was in trouble. Now, I hadn't a clue.

***

"Pass your research notebooks forward, please," Fierce announced Friday afternoon, just before class ended. She collected the thick piles of journals from each row. "I'll read these during the remaining weeks and return them to you before school is out. I expect you did nothing less than your best. Your exhibits at the fair tomorrow count for only part of your grade. The real work is here"—she patted an armload—"in these notebooks."

Several of us exchanged glances. Ha. Fierce would never know *real* work until she had tried to mummify a drippy chicken in less than seven days.

She thunked the notebooks into a large cardboard box,

then faced us with that familiar sharp tug to her blazer. "I expect that your exhibits are completed?"

More exchanged glances. A few nervous coughs.

Our exhibit *would* be ready—if we pulled one more all-nighter.

"Here is your schedule for tomorrow," Fierce went on, handing out bright yellow flyers proclaiming in swirly letters: *The 30th Annual Lemon County Schools History Faire.* She perched atop The Tower. "You will arrive at Hobbs College gym to set up *no later than seven a.m.* You will have two hours to get your exhibits ready. Parent and teacher volunteers will be on hand, if needed, to assist you. I'll be there at six a.m. if any of you would like to start early."

Double ha. We'd probably still be wrapping Cluck in his bandages at 6:01.

"Doors open at nine a.m.," Fierce continued with the speed and intensity of a wildfire. "Students, parents, teachers, librarians, and media from across the county will be admitted at that time. The judging committee begins its tour at nine-fifteen. The superintendent of schools and the mayor will present the awards at ten-thirty. The fair ends at noon. Your projects *must* be removed from the gym no later than one p.m. Are there any questions?"

There weren't.

"Lastly . . ." Fierce's words slowed to a simmer. "Need I remind you of the type of behavior I will find inappropriate tomorrow, or the consequences of that behavior?" She gazed at each of us (except me), letting her words sizzle in. It took her a full silent minute to go around the entire room.

We knew what she was thinking. One baby toe out of line, and we'd fail this class—and end up right back in these seats again next year.

"No, I didn't think so," she finished. Again, the smug smile.

The bell rang. As we gathered our things, she added, her voice almost as kind as it had been when she spoke to Hayley the other night: "We have an excellent chance of winning again this year. The proposals you presented to me weeks ago were superb. I'm looking forward to seeing the results and taking home first prize for the tenth year in a row. See you tomorrow."

***

"Bye, Mom, Dad!" I called upstairs the next morning when I heard the Lickety-Split Chick van honk outside. Mr. Noel, Pierre's dad, owns a fast-food joint featuring home-delivered greasy fried chicken and slushy coleslaw. With all the stuff we were lugging for our portion of the exhibit, we'd needed the biggest car possible, and the delivery van seemed the best bet. The other groups from class would meet us at the gym with the rest of the display.

"See you at nine!" Mom called from the bedroom.

I stopped short, hand reaching for the front doorknob. *"You're coming?"*

I heard the shuffle of slippers. Mom hurried down the stairs, hair sleep-mussed, but her face looking pinker, healthier than it had in weeks. Still no sign of you-know-who beneath her robe, though. "Of course we are!"

"We wouldn't miss seeing one of your great inventions," Dad added, trailing her in his rumpled sweat suit,

"It's not an invention," I insisted, gesturing with King Cluck. *More of a swaddled football–with drumsticks.*

"The idea came from up here, didn't it?" Mom pressed a gentle finger against my forehead. Then she wrinkled her nose. "Stephen J. Wyatt, did you forget to change your underwear this morning?"

"Mom!"

"Well, *something* smells," she said, sniffing my clothes. "Now that you're almost a teenager, I'd better start buying you deodorant."

I shifted King Cluck to my other arm. "I gotta hurry," I said. "We still have to load the van."

"Let me give you a hand," Dad offered. He waved at Mom and closed the door behind us.

"I wanted to thank you for straightening up and flying right these past two weeks," he said as we scuffed through the froth of jasmine blossoms along the walkway. "It was a relief knowing your mother wouldn't have any extra worries." He hunkered down, dialing the combination of the old garage door lock. "I wanted to tell you too how proud we both are of you. Your studying has paid off, hasn't it? Look at all the time and effort you've put into this project! I'm sure this will pull your grade up in Ms. Pierce's class. And soon you'll be winging your way to Patrick Henry. . . no pun intended," he added, with a nod at King Cluck.

My stomach flinched at the mention of high school. If only I could explain to Dad that this project had nothing to do with skipping eighth grade. All I wanted was to make a point to Fierce.

Dad swung open the door. Our exhibit hunched beneath several tarps.

"My group'll carry all this, Dad," I said, not wanting him to peek before the fair. Pierre, Ace, Hayley, and Goldie hopped out of the van. They wore jeans and T-shirts. We'd change into our funeral costumes after we set up the exhibit.

"All right," Dad agreed. "I'll take my shower." He leaned close and murmured: "You should've taken one too, son. Your mother was right: You're giving off a particularly manly odor today. Stay out of crowds, hmm?"

It took a few minutes to squeeze the awkward, bulky project pieces into the back of the van. Then we all piled in and Mr. Noel headed to Hiccup's house to pick up our "oxen."

"Ewww," Goldie complained, pinching her nose and leaning away from me into Ace. "What *reeks?*"

"King Cluck," I answered with a sigh. He was perched on my lap, emanating toxic rot fumes. Mixed with the greasy odor of a bazillion Lickety-Split Chick deliveries, the stench was stomach-turning.

"Mon Dieu!" Pierre rolled down the front passenger window and took great gulps of fresh air. "I can even smell it up here!"

"He's starting to leak through the bandages," Hayley observed.

"I've got some extra in my pack, on the floor."

Hayley rooted around for the linen strips, while Ace opened another window.

"Dredge him in more spices!" Goldie demanded, breathing through her mouth.

"We used them all," I said. "He's gonna smell, and that's all there is to it. One week wasn't enough time to mummify him, and I think the fact that he'd been defrosted didn't help either."

"Zee judges will never give us an award," Pierre grumbled, "if they are barfing into zee sarcophagus!"

"Perhaps," Ace put in calmly, "we'll win for most odiferous exhibit."

"He'll be on display on the burial sled only a little while," I said, holding Cluck so Hayley could wrap a few more bandages around his leakiest under-regions. "Once he's locked inside his tomb, we'll be okay. Mr. Noel, that's Hiccup's house on the left, with the 'Beware of Cat' sign."

I handed King Cluck to Hayley and hurried to the Denardos' front door. Horatio answered, holding out two leashes attached to Dasher and Dancer. They pranced like Santa's reindeer ready to fly, snuffling my hands, serenading me with their most desolate "No one ever feeds us" whine.

"They didn't eat breakfast yet," Horatio explained, handing me a large brown paper bag. "Here's their kibble. They'll need water too, when you get to the school. Oh, and take the pooper-scooper."

"Uh, great, thanks," I said. "I'll bring the dogs home this afternoon."

"Keep 'em!" Hiccup's mom called from inside.

I waved and was yanked down the porch steps. That's when I heard a beautiful, familiar *"HIC!"*

I whirled. Hiccup stood in the doorway.

"*Hector!*" I practically cheered. Only the tangle of D & D's leashes kept me from hugging him. It had been two weeks since I'd last seen him. It felt like two years. He looked pale and thin.

"Man, it's good to see you, buddy!" I said. "What are you doing out here? Aren't you supposed to be resting? Did you get my messages and the get-well card? Your mom wouldn't let me–"

"Wanted *HIC!* say *HIC!* luck."

"Good luck?" I translated. "Thanks, pal." D & D strained against the leash toward the van, almost toppling me over. Then they circled me, licking my fingers. "We're doing King Cluck at the fair. I knew you'd want to know. I'll tell you all about it when you're better."

He nodded. "Hospital *HIC!* week *HIC!* visit?"

"You want me to visit you next week in the hospital?" My stomach squeezed. "You're having those tests, right?"

He nodded again.

"You bet I'll be there," I said. "No. Matter. What."

We stared at each other for a minute. Me blinking, him hicking.

"See you," I said, not knowing what else to say. "See you *soon.*"

He nodded a last time. Then the door shut with a *hic!* and a click.

189

TWENTY-FIVE

DASHER AND DANCER whined the whole way to Hobbs College gym, panting, drooling, and straining to follow Hayley, who, to make room for us, had climbed over the last seat with King Cluck to sit with our exhibit.

Goldie tried to complain when Dasher thumped his rump into her lap, but got a bushy mouthful of tail instead.

"Are they always this *wet?*" Pierre asked. He wiped an unexpected thread of doggie saliva from his shoulder as Dancer investigated his ear canal for food.

"They're hungry," I answered, struggling to keep the leashes from entangling and the dogs from attempting to drive. "And no wonder: Even the seats in here smell like Lickety-Split Chick. We'll feed them as soon as we get to the gym."

Mr. Noel steered onto the freeway. Twenty droolingly uncomfortable minutes later, we arrived at the college. The gym parking lot was packed with idling cars and costumed kids. Two girls dressed in white-faced geisha makeup and kimonos pitter-patted past, carrying what looked like the makings for a Japanese tea ceremony. A group of boys struggled to gingerly transport a giant

190

replica of the Acropolis—made entirely from toothpicks.

"It's after seven, Pierre," Mr. Noel warned. He helped us unload and promised to return at 1:00. "Oh, and don't forget Chicky-Lick." He handed his son the floppy yolk-yellow chicken costume usually worn by a greeter at his restaurant.

"I refuse to wear zees alleged chicken!" Pierre announced with disdain as his dad drove off. "It eez beneath zee dignity of a chef!"

"We've already been through this," I said, impatience filling my voice. "You're not a chef today. You're the pharaoh's brother."

Pierre sniffed.

"Okay, fine. You're in charge of the dogs." I held out their leashes. D & D barked and began licking Pierre's shoes. (Hey, why not? The leather came from an animal that had been meat in a previous life.)

Pierre sighed. "I will wear zee chicken suit. But *never* reveal to a soul that it was me."

D & D towed me across the parking lot. The rest of Group Two followed, toting our project.

An official-looking man with a clipboard stopped us at the main doors of the gym. "Sorry!" he said, holding up his hand. "You can't bring those dogs in here."

"But they're an integral part of our exhibit!" I explained, trying to keep from sounding out of breath as I clung to D & D's leashes. "They're our 'oxen.'"

"Uh-huh."

"No, really. We need them to pull our mummy's funeral sled."

"Saaaaay," Goldie wheedled with a bright smile, nodding at the man's name tag. "Are you *the* Mr. Kelleher? The history teacher from Lemon Valley?"

He straightened his shoulders, returned the smile. "Yes! How'd you know?"

"Oh, my mother, Priscilla Laux, talks about you *all* the time. She's the principal of Jefferson Elementary, and she's always saying how she'd *love* to have someone with your teaching skills on her staff."

Mr. Kelleher blushed. "How nice . . ."

"Now, about our 'oxen' here," Goldie went on. "Our exhibit just *won't* be *historically accurate* without them. Isn't there *any* way you can help us?"

"Well . . ." Mr. Kelleher thought a moment. "Well, all right. You can use the dogs, but you'll have to keep them outside until the very last moment. And one of you will have to stay with them. You can't leave them tied up here alone."

"I'll do it," Hayley said. "Just come get me a few minutes before the funeral procession. I'll need time to change into my costume."

"Why does *she* get to be in the procession!" Goldie said. "She's not even in our class."

"She's our consultant, remember?" I said. "She's worked just as hard, if not harder, than the rest of us this week, so—"

"Hey, Sneeze!" A boy from Group Three, dressed as one of our Egyptian servants, hustled out of the boys' restroom, still adjusting his skirt. "You'd better hurry, man. It's seven-twenty, and Fierce is on the warpath."

"We're coming now!" I swapped the leashes for King Cluck. "Thanks, Hayley," I said. "Thanks for everything."

She nodded.

"Way to go," I whispered to Goldie, for once grateful for her *information*.

We raced inside. Stopped dead in our tracks. Caught our breaths in awe.

The gym had been transformed from a modern sports arena to a Wonder of the Ancient World: There stood the Aztec Calendar. . . Mt. Olympus . . . the Parthenon . . . Mayan temples . . . the Hanging Gardens of Babylon . . . and surrounding them all, the Great Wall of China made out of Popsicle sticks.

"Holy guacamole!" Goldie said.

"Magnifique!" Pierre agreed.

Even Ace arched an eyebrow.

Then all three of them stared at me, accusingly.

"So the competition is stiff," I admitted. "Our project is better. It's the *best*. So stop worrying about what everyone else has done, and let's get set up. There's our spot, in the far corner."

Several kids from our class snaked through the crowds to help us.

"Fierce is sitting in the bleachers," one girl told me, motioning with her head. "Don't look–wow, is she steaming! Teachers aren't allowed to help set up this year. It's supposed to be a totally student-created project. I thought she was going to boil over when we wouldn't let her see what's under the tarps. She calmed down a bit when I told her we want to make an 'entrance' for the judges, that it'll ruin the surprise if the audience sees our exhibit ahead of time."

"Great answer. Perfect," I said.

"What do you want us to do first, Sneeze?" asked a boy from Group One.

I surveyed our exhibit space and made some mental calculations. "Let's put the Nile River over there, our chicken sphinx and tomb right here, and . . ."

"Ladies and gentleman," a voice echoed throughout the gym at exactly nine a.m. "May I have your attention, please?" The mike squealed, people groaned, and the voice tried again. "I'm John Fox, superintendent of Lemon County Schools, and I'd like to welcome you all–teachers, students, librarians, parents, and judges–to our thirtieth annual History Faire!"

Wild applause. Cheers. A few whistles.

"This is it," I said to our class, my stomach somersaulting with excitement. "Goldie, fetch Hayley and the dogs–quick. Sherry, when they get here, you and your group hitch Dasher and Dancer to the sled. Pierre, get into that chicken suit, *now*. No, don't anybody pull the tarps off our exhibit yet. Wait till the judges start their rounds. On second thought, wait till I give the signal. I've got a great idea. Follow my lead–"

Mr. Fox's voice continued to reverberate as he introduced the volunteers and judges. I darted in and out of the exhibits, making my way to the mike. I caught a glimpse of Mom and Dad, sitting in the stands, beaming with pride. I scanned higher to the staff section and spotted Mr. Barker sitting next to Fierce. I almost didn't recognize her. She wore jeans and a white work shirt, a navy sweater tied loosely around her neck. With her hair in a ponytail, one finger in her mouth, she looked more like an anxious student than a disapproving teacher.

I couldn't wait to see her expression when we unveiled our poultry version of the Valley of the Kings . . . couldn't wait to see her face when she realized how much blood, sweat, and feathers we'd put into this project.

" . . . this day wouldn't be possible without our private sponsors," Mr. Fox was saying. "Let's give them a warm Lemon County round of applause!"

More clapping, whistles, and cheers.

"I now declare the History Faire officially open. The judges will begin their rounds in five minutes. Enjoy the morning!" The microphone clicked off. Mr. Fox stepped from the podium just as I reached his side.

"Uh, excuse me, Mr. Fox, sir?" I began. "Hi, I'm Stephen J. Wyatt. From Jefferson Middle School."

"What can I do for you, Mr. Wyatt?" he asked with a smile.

"I was wondering, would it be okay if I use the mike for a minute? My class has a special Egyptian parade planned, and I'd like to announce it."

"Certainly," he agreed. "Push this button right here when you're ready. Make it short, though. Otherwise, we'll have all the other schools clamoring to make announcements too."

"No problem. Thanks."

I took the mike from his hand and stepped onto the

small stage. I peered over the sea of heads and exhibits to my group's corner. Good. Hayley and Pierre wore their costumes. Dasher and Dancer had been hitched to the sled. The rest of the class, dressed as mourners and servants in chicken beaks, lined up behind it. I caught Ace's attention, and flashed him a thumbs-up.

He nodded and nudged several kids. Together, they whisked off the tarps and sheets. Our exhibit gleamed, bejeweled and befeathered, under the bright lights of the gym. The audience gasped.

I switched on the mike. "G-good morning," I began nervously. The buzz of voices quieted. "I'd like to direct your attention to the far corner, where Ms. Daisy Pierce's class from Jefferson Middle School opens its exhibit with a re-creation of an ancient Egyptian funeral!"

Ace tapped Dasher and Dancer on their bottoms with a stick. They giddyupped to circle the gym, towing the funeral sled with the empty sarcophagus. The royal court and a line of mourners followed.

"Our great and wise pharaoh, King Cluck," I announced, "has died suddenly in his roost after a reign of twenty-seven years. He leaves his devoted family, servants, and subjects bereft."

The mourners, as they plodded past the stands, began clucking and squawking in grief. Chicky-Lick flapped his wings. Cleopecktra wailed, tearing at her feathers.

I heard a few titters and giggles from the audience.

The "servants" paraded by next, their faces stoic as they carried nests and chests filled with Cluck's belongings.

"On the day of King Cluck's funeral, as is the custom," I continued, "a procession of mourners begins the pharaoh's journey to the afterlife at his palace—er, coop."

More chuckles.

"An elaborate empty coffin is placed on a wooden sled and pulled by oxen"—Dasher and Dancer barked; the audience laughed—"to the City of the Dead. This is where the embalmers have toiled, lo, these last forty days, to mummify the king. The mummified pharaoh is placed in his coffin, or sarcophagus, and taken to the Valley of the Kings for a magnificent funeral feast. He will attend this banquet, given in his honor, before his entombment."

My last words were drowned out by more laughter. This wasn't exactly the reaction I expected . . .

Hayley, dressed as a priestess, held Cluck aloft for the audience to see. People sputtered. Chortled. She seemed not to notice, and moved with elegance in her gown around Dasher and Dancer to place Cluck reverently into his coffin.

D & D stiffened in Red Alert. Each strand of hair on their thick bodies, from the tips of their tails to the nips of their ears, twitched and trembled. Their noses jerked into the air, snuffling hard at a mystery aroma in Hayley's wake. Dasher whirled to the right, Dancer, to the left. They bonked into each other, yelped, reversed direction, trying to follow the scent. The sled overturned and whipped behind them so hard and fast that King Cluck went flying, up, up, into the air, spinning over and over like a football soaring toward the end zone.

That's when it hit me. The greasy smell of the Lickety-

Split Chick van wasn't what had gotten D & D riled up. It had been the rotting, reeking, putrid poultry odor of—

"King Cluck!" I yelled into the microphone. "Save him!"

Ace leaped high and scooped Cluck under his arm. He turned and his eyebrows soared as he saw D & D bearing down on him.

"RUN!" I shouted.

Ace about-faced and charged as if hurtling for a touch-down, zigging and zagging round students, through exhibits. Dasher and Dancer pursued—tongues lolling, eyes exuberant, paws scrambling against the slick polished floor—dragging the sled behind them.

Kids shouted. Screamed. Leaped out of the way. The audience was on its feet, laughing, cursing, shouting garbled instructions.

Ace couldn't hear. He dodged on toward the exit, the dogs gaining, tails thrashing, paws a blur, the sled careening, crashing into and bouncing off exhibits. In seconds, Dasher and Dancer had rototilled the Hanging Gardens of Babylon . . . toppled the Leaning Tower of Pisa . . . demolished the Mayan temple . . . crumpled the Japanese origami . . . and set the Great Wall of China cascading to the floor like a row of dominoes.

The dogs finally tackled Ace by the drinking fountains. He clutched Cluck close to his body, but they wrenched it from his arms, gleefully tearing at the bandages, munching on the bones, while the crowd continued to shriek and scream and laugh.

Hayley scrambled up to me, her face twisted in horror.

"I'm so sorry, Steve, sorry!" she babbled through the cacophony of chaos.

I shook my head. It wasn't her fault. It was mine. I'd forgotten to give her the bag of dog food. Worse, I'd tried to get away with bad science. I hadn't allowed enough time for Cluck to mummify—and that decision had ruined everything.

Hayley rushed to help Ace to his feet. Two teachers tried to push D & D outside. Students wandered through the debris of their trampled exhibits, their mouths slack with shock.

I couldn't look. Couldn't watch. I turned away, stumbled off the podium, smack into—

Fierce.

Her ponytail had come loose. Tears streaked her freckles. Her green eyes grilled into me.

She thinks I've done this on purpose to humiliate her, I realized with a plunging of my stomach, *to get back at her for Hiccup and the Death Roll and—*

"Ms. Pierce!" I began. "I didn't want—"

"Are you happy now?" she demanded, her voice thick, sad. She swiped at the tears, pushed past me, and ran out of the gym.

TWENTY-SIX

*ATTILA THE HEN Attacks Student History Faire . . .
Paltry Poultry Experiment Blamed for Fowl-Up . . . Chicken
Project Lays Egg*

On Sunday, the disaster at Hobbs gym made the front
page of three Lemon County newspapers. I know
because Goldie called to quote each headline aloud
before slamming down the phone.

I didn't bother to read the articles. I'd already experienced the cyclonic aftermath of that morning firsthand—
or, rather, firstwing.

After the dust and glitter and feathers had settled, and
the crowds ushered out, our class stayed behind to
restore the gym. Mom, Dad, and Mr. Barker helped too.
It took us three hours to sweep, shovel, and pitch five
thousand years of history into the school Dumpsters.

Hayley stayed at my side in her askewed priestess costume the entire time. Every now and then she gave my
arm a squeeze and said: "It's gonna be okay, Steve.
Honest." Not one other student spoke to me while we
worked. They didn't have to. Their glares, frowns, scowls,
and tears said it all.

I'd blown it again. Let them down. They'd expected so

much, and I hadn't delivered. I owed them, and I owed them big. Especially now that we'd all get F's in Fierce's class—and be doomed to repeat world history with her.

When the gym looked neat and clean again, Goldie, Pierre, and Ace sped off in Mr. Noel's van without a backward glance. "I'll call you later," Hayley whispered, before heading home with her dad. I loaded Dasher and Dancer into Dad's convertible, where they promptly barfed half-digested chicken bits and strings of slimy bandages all over the backseat.

Mom clapped a hand to her mouth and looked away, but Dad just laughed. He gave me a wad of napkins from the glove compartment and leaned against the dashboard, laughing and gulping and laughing some more.

"David!" Mom admonished. "It's not funny!"

"Yes, it is," he chortled, verging on hysterics. "Well, I know it's not, really. But I keep picturing that chicken, soaring through the air . . . Dasher and Dancer erupting out of the top of Mount Vesuvius, and . . . and . . . OH!" He wiped at his eyes and tried to swallow his chuckles, but broke into a groan of laughter again, his shoulders heaving.

Mom crossed her arms. "Think of your son, David. You're being totally insensitive."

Dad coughed. Cleared his throat. Wiped his eyes once more, and turned to find me swabbing at the chicken bits while D & D tried to re-eat them. "You're right. I'm sorry, Steve. But sometimes laughter is better than the alternative." He got out of the car to help me wipe up the chicky chunks. When we'd finished and thrown the mess in the trash, he placed both hands on my shoulders and looked me in the eye. "Seriously, son, you worked tremendously hard on this project. And, despite the, uh, outcome, it was a brilliant one. It wasn't the wisest of decisions getting these two"–he gestured at the dogs–"omnivorous beasts involved. But, still, you did your best. And that's what counts."

But I hadn't done my best, I thought as we drove home. I'd known from the start that what I'd done was bad science. King Cluck needed at least four to six weeks to completely mummify; I tried to do it in one, just to prove a point.

What had it gotten me?

A teacher who hated me.

A teacher who thought I'd caused the disaster to embarrass her in front of the superintendent and every history teacher in the county.

A teacher whose belief that all middle-school kids were hoodlums had just been confirmed.

I couldn't do anything to erase her humiliation. I couldn't do anything to change how she felt about me.

But there was one thing, one last thing I could try, to change her feelings about my fellow students.

***

Monday morning I slipped out the door to pedal to school before 7:00 A.M. Rumor had it that Fierce could always be found working in her classroom an hour before first bell.

My sneakers squeaked down the empty, newly-waxed floor of the main hall. My stomach squeaked too, like chickens were peck-pecking inside of it.

"Sneeze?"

I heard the familiar drawl behind me. Tony stood there, unlocking the door to the nurse's office with a lasso of keys that jangled like spurs.

"Hey, Tony," I said.

"I read about what happened," he went on, his voice calm and slow. "I'm not gonna ask how you are, 'cuz I think we both know that's a stupid question."

I shrugged.

"Like to come in and tell me about it? I can rustle up a cup of hot chocolate."

"No, thanks, Tony. There's nothing to tell. Except— well, after what happened on Saturday, I know now that I've made the right decision."

His caterpillar-brows scooted upward. "What decision is that?"

"To quit inventing."

"Ah." He pocketed his keys. Opened his door. "And you think that's the solution, do ya?"

I shrugged again.

"That's your decision to make, of course," he said. "But I gotta tell ya, when a horse bucks you off, you gotta climb right back on again. If you still love her. If you still love the ride." He disappeared into his office, leaving the door ajar.

I ignored the invitation, and continued toward Fierce's class.

I found her seated behind her desk, surrounded by mounds of open notebooks—our history project note-books. A pair of glasses sat perched on the end of her nose. Her hair was pulled back again in its ponytail; loose strands wisped across her cheeks.

"Ms. Pierce?" I began.

She jumped, startled. "Mr. Wyatt . . ."

She whisked off her glasses, clutching them in a fist. Her eyes looked red. "What can I do for you?"

I stood at the edge of her desk, directly in front of her, directly in front of the Death Roll box, like a criminal standing before a judge.

"I wanted to tell you I'm sorry," I said. "And to explain about Saturday." I took a deep breath, and the words tumbled out. "I know you think that I did it on purpose. That *we* did it on purpose. To get back at you. To hurt you. But that's not true. We worked really hard on our project—as a team. Our whole class. Well, everyone except Hiccup, and he would've if he could've, you know . . ."

I stopped. Swallowed. Thought about my friend, how he'd been hicking constantly since the Day of the Death Roll. How he hadn't deserved that. None of us had.

"We . . ." I continued, "Well, no, I wanted to show you how smart we are, how we could work without threats. How we deserved to work without threats and without punishments that . . . that humiliate us . . ."

Fierce's gaze flickered to the notebooks. I kept going.

"That's why I came up with the chicken mummy funeral, and convinced the class they should go along with it. To impress you. To make you understand. It wasn't their fault King Cluck wasn't ready, that he wasn't completely mummified. It was *my* fault. That's why the dogs went after him. That's why everything went wrong. Because of me. So you shouldn't give Goldie or Pierre or anyone else in class an F, or make them take this course over again. They worked really hard. They've learned their Egyptian history. Honest."

"I know," Fierce said.

They were the last words I expected her to utter at that moment.

"You—*know?*"

She sighed, nodded, then shook her head. "I can't say I wasn't angry and embarrassed at first, Mr. Wyatt. I was ready to demote the entire class straight back to the first grade. For making a fool out of me, for making a mockery of our exhibit." She slipped her glasses on again. "But then I came in here. I spent all day yesterday reading through your notebooks. All of them. I've just finished."

She surveyed the piles of colorful notebooks stretched out around her. "As I said last Friday, this is where the real work is. And to my surprise, despite the gym disaster, it's true. Every single notebook is impeccable. The research is thorough. The projects, historically accurate. The ideas, clever. I've never seen such fine work, not in ten years of teaching at this school."

I gulped. "Then—you're not—going to flunk us? *None* of us?"

"Not even you, Mr. Wyatt," she admitted wryly. "Of course, it goes without saying we didn't win first prize. I doubt our school will be allowed to compete next year, if ever again. But that's not the end of the world—even though, perhaps, it feels like it—because we all learned something. A lot of somethings. That's what's important. The rest is just . . ." She smiled, and her green eyes seemed cool and serene for the very first time. "The rest is just . . . chicken feed."

TWENTY-SEVEN

WHEN FIERCE ANNOUNCED that afternoon in fifth period that none of us would fail her class, you could've heard a feather drop.

Goldie's mouth plummeted. Pierre's beret slid, unnoticed, to the floor. Ace arched *both* eyebrows (which for anyone else would've been the equivalent of an electric shock).

The other students sat stunned, silent, at the unbelievable good news.

Of course, that news didn't come without its consequences. Fierce proceeded to rant and riot at us for fifteen solid minutes—about irresponsible choices, rash decisions, and our disgraceful portrayal of an Egyptian monarch.

But, as Goldie pointed out when we skulked through the door at the end of class, perhaps Fierce wasn't as angry as she'd led us to believe. "Didn't you notice?" she demanded, nudging me with a sharp elbow. "On her desk? Sneeze, it's *gone!*"

"What's gone?" I asked.

"The Death Roll box! The chart's gone too. They're in the *trash.*" Goldie tapped sparkly nails against her teeth. "I wonder why. That's the information I want. What–or who–made her get rid of them?"

I arranged my face to look as innocent as possible. "I haven't a clue," I said.

***

I didn't tell Hiccup about the History Faire disaster for three reasons: 1) I knew he'd feel responsible for the Random Acts of Eating his dogs had performed; 2) He had enough to hic about with all those hospital tests coming up; 3) Mrs. Denardo still wouldn't let me see or talk to him.

"And under no circumstances," she'd said when I returned D & D, "will you be allowed to visit Hector in the hospital."

"But he asked me to!" I replied. "He wants me there. I want to be there. I'm his best friend!"

"A hospital is not for socializing," she insisted. "Besides, every time you two are together, he hics worse than ever. I'll call you when he's home. That's final."

But it wasn't final for me. I told Mom what Mrs. Denardo said, and asked if she'd call Hic's mom on my behalf.

"Good news!" Mom sang, knocking on my bedroom door Wednesday night. I had just blearily turned out the light and climbed into bed after finishing the two hours of nightly homework Fierce had assigned us.

"Did you talk to her? Can I see him?" I asked.

Mom nodded and sat on the edge of my bed, smoothing the comforter with her long, slender fingers. "It's all arranged. Mrs. Denardo is willing to allow a visit before

Hiccup's first test. Only for an hour, and only if you promise not to talk about school or anything else that might upset him."

I scooted bolt upright. "Of course! Anything! Whatever she wants!"

"Good. My amniocentesis is scheduled tomorrow morning at nine at the same hospital. You may come with Dad and me, and visit with Hiccup while I have the test. We'll take you to school after that, all right?"

"Thanks, Mom," I said, and hugged her.

"You're welcome, honey. Sleep tight." She stood to go— then stopped. By the moon-glow of the aquarium, I could just barely make out her face: brows pinched, lips in a twitch of worry as she gazed at the empty maze of shelves.

"Steve?" she whispered. "What—what's happened to all your inventions?"

I sunk deep into the comforter. "I put them away. I told you, remember? I'm not an inventor anymore."

"But why? What happened?"

I shrugged. "Nothing. I've just got . . . other things on my mind right now."

"Would you like to talk about it?"

"No. Not . . . yet."

"Soon?"

"Maybe."

She kissed me on the forehead. "It'll be all right, Steve," she said.

"What will?" I asked. "Hiccup?"

"Everything," she murmured, and padded out the door.

The next morning, we arrived at the Lemon County Hospital a few minutes before nine. I bought Hiccup a couple of his favorite comic books in the gift shop, then Mom and Dad showed me the waiting room on the fourth floor where I would meet them after my visit. Hand in hand, they hurried to the check-in desk where a sign read: *Obstetrics Department–Perinatal Unit.*

I waved to them as the elevator doors closed, punched the eighth-floor Pediatrics button, and breathed through my mouth during the quick ride. The sharp hospital smell of alcohol, pine-scented floor wax, and overcooked cafeteria stew was worse, in my opinion, than a rotting King Cluck.

"Hey, Hic!" I said peering into his room. He was lying in a bed with criblike rails, propped against a pile of snowy-white pillows.

"*Hic!*-lo!" he replied with an excited smile. He motioned for me to come in. He wore a thin white hospital gown with blue bunnies on it, his arms poking out like sticks. Medical journals were spread across his flannel blanket. The bed next to his was empty, probably because his torturous *hic-hic-hicking* would drive any roomie screaming to the Psychiatric Ward.

"Mom *hic!* just *hic!* left," he struggled to say. "Get *hic!* coffee."

Good. I felt nervous enough without Mrs. Denardo here to monitor my every cough, breath, or blink for something stress-inducing for her son.

"These are for you." I thrust the comics into Hiccup's hands.

He nodded in thanks. "How *hic!* was *hic!* fair?"

"Oh, um, educational," I answered. "I'll tell you all about it after you're home. Say, this is a really nice room! You've got your own tissue box and water pitcher and everything!"

I pretended to be fascinated by the view out his window (a red rooftop with a rusty air conditioner) and a scattering of belongings on the shelf under the TV (his old teddy bear, Dr. Salk; a framed sketch of Medicine Man; his humidifier). There weren't any flowers (Hiccup is allergic to pollen) or balloons (ditto, latex), but displayed on his dresser were get-well cards from Hayley, me, his grandma, and one "signed" by all eight Denardo dogs.

"Hey, who's this from?" I'd spotted a silver mylar balloon on a stick, hidden behind the drapes as if the giver was too embarrassed to have it seen. The balloon, with a cutesy puppy on the front, was jammed into a Styrofoam cup filled with dirt. A message read: *Hope you feel doggone grrrrrrreat again soon!*

"Who's this from?" I repeated.

Hiccup frowned like he'd never seen it before. "Don't *hic!* know."

I lifted the cup to check for a get-well card. Beneath it, on the windowsill, was a playing card. No note. No signature. Just an ace of spades.

"That's weird," I said.

A nurse bustled in to take Hic's blood pressure and temperature. She jotted notes on a clipboard, patted his shoulder, and said: "Hang in there, Hector, dear. The orderly will be here soon to take you for your MRI. Your chart says you have claustrophobia. The MRI tube is a tight fit, so I'll be back in a moment to give you a sedative." She hustled from the room.

"Maybe I should go," I said, edging toward the door.

"You just *HIC!* got here!"

"I know, but–"

"Don't!" Hiccup's eyes ovaled wide like hard-boiled eggs.

"What's wrong?" I asked.

"I'm *HIC! HIC!* scared."

"I'd be scared too." I swept the comic books aside and thumped down next to his feet. "I *am* scared!"

He glanced at the get-well cards, then out the window at the rusty air conditioner. Tears filled his eyes.

My insides felt ripped, shredded. I leaped to my feet and paced the small room. "Man, I hate this!" I said, my fists clenching and unclenching. "If only there was something I could do! If only I could invent again! Hector, believe me, I'd work night and day until I built the biggest and best Hiccup Inhibitor the world has ever seen! Then you wouldn't need the MBA and EEK or whatever they're called!"

He hic-nodded. Half laughed. Wiped at his eyes.

"Isn't there *something* the doctors can do besides all these scary tests?" I was still pacing. "A treatment they haven't tried yet? A drug or exercise or . . . maybe hypnosis! Or something that's worked in the past that they forgot about, huh? Come on, Hiccup! The clock is ticking! Think. You've been getting hiccups for years. Never this bad, but what stopped them before?"

He plucked at his blanket. "Only *hic!* Her," he said finally.

"Her? Oh, you mean Mom. That's right. Looking at her used to stop your hiccups cold. But you saw Mom just a few weeks ago, the night she had the, uh, flu. Seeing her didn't faze your hiccups one bit."

Hiccup shook his head. "Didn't *hic!* see *hic!* Her."

"Of course you saw her," I replied. "Remember? I told you she was sick, and you raced up to her bedroom to . . ."

Like a tape recorder, I rewound the scene in my mind. Watched the memory movie of Hiccup wrenching open the door. Me, scrambling to stop him, bumping into him in the dark. A hump in Mom's bed, grumbling: *Turn on that light and you're dead men.*

We never turned on the light. We never saw Mom's face.

Hiccup never saw Mom's face.

"Get up!" I cried. "Get out of bed. Now!"

I dashed into the hall. Spied a lone wheelchair, near the restroom. Snagged it. Zoomed it into Hic's room.

"Get in," I said. "Quick!"

Hiccup hadn't moved.

"Where *HIC!* going?"

"To see Mom," I said, urging him to sit up.

"She is *hic!* here? She is *hic!* ill?" His face paled white as his pillows.

"She's pregnant. She's downstairs having a test. An ambivalent . . . no, that's not right. An amino acid? No . . ."

"Amni—*hic!*—ocen—*hic!*—tesis?"

"Yeah! Now get into the chair, otherwise we'll look

212

suspicious." I grabbed the blanket from Hic's bed and threw it over his legs. "Here we go . . ."

I wheeled him to the doorway. Peeked into the hall. No sign of the nurse with the sedative. Or the orderly. A uniformed lady at the nurses' station peered into a computer monitor. I took a deep breath, and pushed Hiccup in the opposite direction, toward the elevators.

Hic hiccupped with anxiety and excitement.

"Try to keep it down," I muttered, pulling the blanket up over his mouth.

I reached the elevators. Stabbed the Down buttons on both of them. Tapped my foot. Glanced over my shoulder.

"C'mon, c'mon," I whispered.

"Hic! Hic!" said Hiccup.

A man carting a mop emerged from the utility room. At the same moment, Hiccup's nurse, carrying a small tray, stepped into the hall. They stopped to chat. I held my breath.

Ping!

Both elevators opened. I pushed Hiccup into the empty one, passing Mrs. Denardo as she came out of the other.

Hiccup waved at her. "Hi *hic!* Mom!"

She smiled at us–then froze.

"Wait!" she hollered. "Where are you going with my son! Stop! Nurse? Nurse! HELP!"

Hiccup's nurse came running.

"Push Four, push Four!" I yelled at Hiccup, who was closest to the panel. He bashed the button.

"Uh, we'll be right back, Mrs. Denardo!" I said as our

doors closed. I glimpsed a blur of her and the nurse, charging into the other elevator. Our car lurched downward.

"Oh, man," I said, wiping my forehead. "I'm going to have dog status with your mom the rest of my life!"

The doors opened. We started out.

I heard Mrs. Denardo's elevator *ping* open behind us.

I skidded the wheelchair into the hall. Zigzagged past two pregnant ladies. Swooped around a woman in a doctor's coat.

"*HIC!*–whoa!" cried Hiccup, gripping the arms of his chair.

"Where's my mom?" I shouted at a run to the nurse at the Obstetrics desk.

"What's her name, dear?" she asked, not looking up.

"Mrs. Wyatt! I need to see her right away. It's an emergency!"

"Room seven, dear, but you can't go in there—"

"Stop that wheelchair!" Hiccup's nurse cried.

"He's got my son!" screamed Mrs. Denardo.

I barreled toward room 7, Hiccup covering his eyes as we took a corner on one wheel.

"Mom!" I cried, wrenching open the door, charging blindly into a darkened room. It was lit in only one corner by the glow of computer screen. A small figure that looked sort of like a fish spine rippled and bobbed on the screen. A doctor working at the terminal turned to stare.

Mom lay on an exam table, Dad holding her hand.

"What's the meaning of this?" demanded the doctor.

"Son!" Dad said.

214

"Stephen!" Mom cried.

"Dr. Oakes!" yelled the nurse.

"Hec-*tor*!" screeched Mrs. Denardo.

"Hiccup?" said Mom.

"Mrs. *hic!* Wyatt?" he asked with a trace of disbelief, and uncovered his eyes.

Mom raised herself up on her elbows. Her white hospital gown looked like the dress of an angel. The glow from the terminal framed her beautiful, joyful face in a halo.

"Well, as long as you're here, Steve, Hiccup"–she gave a little laugh–"I'd like to introduce you to"–she pointed to the screen–"your baby sister."

"Sister?" I said.

Hiccup gazed first at Mom and then at the screen with unflinching adoration and joy.

"HIC-*ahhhhhhhh*!" he replied.

TWENTY-EIGHT

"HICCUP!" I SAID, my voice hushed so as not to startle him. "Your hiccups are . . . *gone*."

"They *are*?" My friend sucked in a breath and cocked his head as if to better hear over the sudden silence that rocked the room.

Five seconds passed.

Then ten.

Twenty.

Forty-five . . .

Hiccup let out the breath. "You are undoubtedly correct, Sneeze." He grinned.

I grinned back so wide, I thought my smile muscles would snap like a rubber band.

"It's a miracle!" Mrs. Denardo cried, clasping her hands.

"No," I said with a laugh. "It's Mom."

Hiccup leaped Medicine Man–style to Mom's side, where he fussed to tuck the sheet in around her.

"Are you warm enough, Mrs. Wyatt?" he asked. He eyed the doctor with suspicion. "Was the ultrasound gel heated before she applied it to your abdomen? It is a courtesy that takes little time and makes the mother-to-be more comfortable."

Mom chuckled. "Oh, Hiccup. Dear, dear Hiccup." She reached out with both arms to pat his worried face, to squeeze my hand. "I'm very comfortable. Even more so now that my boys are with me!"

"You named your children *Sneeze and Hiccup*?" the doctor asked. She gestured at the computer screen, where the fish-skeleton image still rippled. "What will this little gal be called, then? *Cough*?"

"We haven't chosen a name for the baby yet," Dad put in. "And Hiccup isn't *our* son. He's hers." He nodded toward Mrs. Denardo, who still stood staring in shock at the hiccup-less Hiccup. "As for the nicknames, well, never mind. Dr. Oakes, may I introduce our son, Stephen?"

"A pleasure," she said, with a flash of smile. Then her face turned doctorly again. "You may stay, if you like. The rest of you out—now!"

Hiccup's nurse sniffed. "Yes, Doctor. This boy is scheduled for an MRI in five minutes, anyway. I'll see that he's taken back to his room immediately." She grasped the wheelchair. "Please sit down, Hector."

"The MRI and other tests are no longer warranted," Hiccup announced. "My hiccups have gone. I am needed here."

"You're needed upstairs, in your bed," the nurse replied. "Only your doctor can determine if the tests should be canceled."

Hiccup bristled, but Mom patted his cheek and said, "Don't worry, Hector. I'm in good hands. Steve and Mr. Wyatt will keep Dr. Oakes on her toes. We'll be up to see you as soon as we're finished."

217

"Agreed," he said with a last, distrustful glance at the doctor. I had the feeling he would insist on making a pit stop at Dr. Oakes's office so he could examine her medical degrees to make sure they weren't the mail-order kind.

"Thanks, Sneeze," he added. He raised his hand and flashed Medicine Man's TJV sign.

"Anytime," I said, returning the sign and his grin.

The nurse pushed Hector out of the room, followed by Mrs. Denardo.

The door closed.

"Now where were we?" Dr. Oakes murmured. "Oh, yes, the ultrasound."

"What about that special test?" I asked. "Have you done it yet?"

"All finished," Dad said. "We've just been watching your little sister swim around. She's a pollywog after my own heart!"

"But how is she? The baby, I mean." I peered at the ultrasound screen, my stomach imitating her wriggles. "She looks like a fish. She's not going to have gills, is she? Is she okay? What did the test say?"

Dr. Oakes fiddled with a dial on the machine. "We won't have the results back for a week, Stephen. But so far, everything looks great. Little, uh, *Cough* should be making her debut in about seven months. And following in her brother's inventor footsteps, from what I hear." She smiled. "I'll be back in a few minutes. Mrs. Wyatt, you may get dressed whenever you're ready."

As soon as the doctor had hurried from the room, I said: "You *told* her?" Anger swelled my voice. "You told a

218

stranger I'm an inventor, even after I swore to you that I'm not?"

"Dr. Oakes isn't exactly a stranger, Steve," Dad said. "She's been your mom's doctor for several years. She has a daughter who'll enter Patrick Henry in the fall, just like you. She's interested in the sciences too. Perhaps you'll be in a few of the same classes and—"

"Stop!" I blurted, putting my hands over my ears. "I'm not going to high school next year. I'm *not*!"

"Since when?" Dad asked.

"Since always!" I whirled away. "I'm not what you think I am. I'm not what you expect me to be. My sister is not going to follow in my inventor footsteps, because I'm not an inventor anymore!"

"Since when?" Dad asked.

"Since—" My voice caught. I took a deep breath. Turned to face them. I shoved out the words. "Since I got inventor's block five months ago."

There. I'd done it. I'd said it. Somehow, what I'd been so afraid of wasn't as scary, now that I'd let it out to my parents.

"Why didn't you tell us?" Mom murmured. "We could've talked about it, helped you with—"

"I couldn't tell you," I admitted. "I was afraid you'd be mad. Disappointed."

Dad shook his head.

Mom looked as if she might cry. "Oh, honey, I'm so sorry . . ."

"It's okay," I said. "It's okay that I can't invent. I—I don't want to anymore."

"It's not that!" Mom sat up, leaned toward me. "I'm sorry we put so much pressure on you. Sorry we gave you the impression that your inventions were all we cared about. Home should be a safe place, where you can talk to us about your problems without fearing you'll let us down!"

"We just wanted what was best for you," Dad said. "We thought that was Patrick Henry. But we don't want you to go just to please us. We don't want you living your life to please anyone—except yourself."

Mom reached out for me, tugged me close. "Stephen J. Wyatt, now hear this!" she said. "If you don't want to go to Patrick Henry, that's fine with us. If you never want to invent another gadget again, that's fine with us too. We love you. No. Matter. What. Got it?"

I took a deep breath and smiled into her eyes. "Got it," I answered.

But there was one thing I didn't get. One thing I wasn't sure about. I didn't know if never wanting to invent again was really, truly, definitely fine with *me*.

TWENTY-NINE

FRIDAY.

Leap-and-laugh-like-it's-your-birthday day.

The day Hiccup was released from the hospital.

The doctors had kept him overnight for observation, just in case his hiccups returned. They hadn't. I had the feeling he might never get them again.

At the tender age of twelve, my friend had already hicked a lifetime's worth.

And, in the coming months, he was much too busy fussing over Mom and my future sister—investigating the latest immunizations for babies; designing a mural of pink cartoon characters to stencil on the nursery (my room!) walls; popping by each morning to make sure Mom took her prenatal vitamins—to stress about anything else.

That Friday felt like ten birthdays all rolled into one for another reason: Hayley gave me my old job back at Gadabout Golf.

"I can't believe you're going to have a baby sister!" Hayley greeted me when I reported for duty after school. I found her seated on the edge of London Bridge, dangling her feet over the murky river Thames.

I plunked beside her, tossing a stone at the speaker system tucked behind a tuft of reeds to get the frog recording to croak again.

"I can't believe I'm back—for good." I closed my eyes and sucked in a great gulp of Gadabout. "Man, I love this place."

"As soon as your sis can walk, we'll teach her how to play miniature golf," Hayley said. "I wonder if there's a company that makes putters for toddlers. Oh, and she can use my hiding place in the Great Pyramid! Maybe turn it into a clubhouse for her friends, a place where they can keep secrets, share secrets."

"Won't you need it anymore?" I asked.

"Huh. Don't you think I'm getting too old for something like that?"

I smiled and tossed a bigger rock at the speaker. The "frogs" burped in protest, then began a gravelly chorus.

"What's going on with Fierce and your dad?" I asked. "Are they still dating?"

"Yeah, but maybe not for long." Hayley curved a strand of hair behind one ear. "Daddy said she's taking a sabbatical from teaching next year to—how did he put it?— 'rethink her future in the field of education.' She's going to Egypt this summer too. She's been teaching Egyptian history for ten years, and she's never been there, can you imagine?"

"I wonder if she'll ever look at a mummy without thinking about Cluck," I said.

Hayley laughed. "I wonder if she'll ever eat chicken again!" She stood and dusted off her jeans. "Hey, let's you, me, and Hiccup do something tomorrow to celebrate.

Hic's out of the hospital, you're back at Gadabout, you don't have to go to Patrick Henry if you don't want to . . . what do you think?"

"I think yes."

"So what should we do? Go to the beach? The movies? Pizza?"

I took another great gulp of Gadabout. Soaked in the sight of the Windmill vanes circling . . . Big Ben tick-tocking away . . . Ol' Faithful spewing faithfully into the used car lot. All holes I had repaired, tinkered with, improved on. . .

"What would you think," I said, "about going to the Invention Convention® with me?"

Hayley's breath caught. "This is kinda sudden, isn't it?"

I shrugged.

"Does this mean you want to invent again?"

I shrugged once more. "I don't know. Maybe I just want to get some ideas to improve Gadabout. Maybe I'm just curious to see what invention July and the Amys finally came up with."

"Huh," Hayley said, arms crossed, the SOS on Orange Alert. But she smiled. A hopeful smile. "Then let's all three of us go."

***

"So, you've returned to the scene of the crime, eh?" asked Mr. Kelleher, the history teacher who'd barred our way at the doors of Hobbs gym the previous Saturday. "Wait, I'd better frisk you just in case you're carrying any nutrition-deprived dogs!" He slapped a leg and laughed.

Hayley snorted as Mr. Kelleher let us pass.

"What did he mean?" Hiccup asked.

"I'll tell you some other time."

The gym looked completely different today. Instead of ancient architectural wonders, the squeaky, polished floor was filled with a myriad of mechanical devices and gadgets and gizmos. We wandered up and down the aisles, watching as students proudly demonstrated a hair-cutting machine, an automatic sock-sorter, a toilet seat with landing lights, an electric nose mitten, a doggie doorbell, and more.

"How does this make you feel?" Hayley asked as we meandered. "Seeing all these creations?"

"Some look silly, some of them have lots of potential," I answered.

"Perhaps you misheard the question," Hiccup said. "Hayley did not query as to your *thoughts* about the inventions, but to your *feelings.*"

"I don't know how I feel," I admitted, shoving my hands into my pockets. "I was hoping I'd feel excited. Inspired. But I only feel . . . numb."

Hayley sighed.

"Stephen, Hector! Howdy, pardners," came a drawl from behind us. A friendly hand clapped my shoulder.

Tony smiled at us from under a ten-gallon hat. He pulled Hiccup into a bear hug. While Hic went rosy beneath his freckles, Tony tipped his hat to Hayley, saying, "Ma'am.

"Glad to see ya, Hic," he went on. "Lots of us were mighty worried about you. How ya doin'?"

"Aside from a slight protein depletion and a temporary case of acid reflux, I am well," Hiccup replied.

"Maybe next week you'll tell me all about the nursin' staff at the hospital."

"Are you one of the teacher volunteers today?" I asked.

"Yessir. And I was pleased to see you're back in the saddle."

"What do you mean?"

"Your booth. With the Nice Alarm. Haven't you been there yet?" Tony plucked a folded exhibit map from his boot. "Aisle eight, space twenty-two. Thataway."

"It's a mistake," I said. "I pulled the Nice Alarm from the competition, remember?"

Tony tilted his hat and studied me from beneath his bushy caterpillar brows. "I think you'd better see for yourself," he said, his voice low, concerned. Then he turned to help a family from Hershey Junior High wanting to locate the Bed-Head Begone device.

Hiccup and Hayley followed me to aisle 8, space 22. A powder blue tablecloth with puffy white clouds covered the exhibit table. The Amys, dressed in sparkly game show hostess gowns, posed, beaming, on either side of a placard reading: *I've Got An Idea! Jefferson Middle School Inventor's Club.* Displayed in front of the placard perched the Nice Alarm.

My Nice Alarm.

Well, not exactly. It was a crude copy, a half-baked imitation, with sequins and sparkles to match the Amys' dresses. Pinned to the clock's arm, like a blooming corsage, was a green ribbon. The Nice Alarm was a finalist in the Household Inventions Division.

The Amys' pasted-on smiles melted like hot glue when they saw me.

"Uh-oh," said the Amys.

"Uh-oh," the Amys said. "What are *you* doing here?"

"What are *you* doing with my alarm?" I demanded.

July arrived, swooping over in a swirl of cape.

"Oh," she said, plunking down three cups of juice. One corner of her mouth lifted in an unconcerned smile.

"'Oh'"? I repeated. "You *steal* my idea and all you can say is *'Oh'*"?

Kids from the next exhibit turned to stare.

"Keep your voice down," soothed July. She sailed behind the table, placing a protective, elegant hand on the alarm. "You didn't leave me a choice, Sneeze. It was too late to build another entry. Our school would've been disqualified."

"But you've taken credit for *my* invention!"

"Do you have any proof it's yours?" July asked. "Your invention journals are gone. There's no record anywhere that you built the original alarm."

Hayley leaned across the table, her SOS an inch from July's face. "Hiccup and I know it's Steve's invention," she said. "He built it, by himself, over a year ago. We'll tell the judges. And the Invention Convention® committee. And–"

"And just who do you think they'll believe?" July said. "I'm a straight-A student! I'm Queen of the Clubs! I'm about to be accepted to the most prestigious high school in all of southern California!"

"Wait. One. Minute." I said. "How did you know my invention journals are gone? Did you take *them* too . . . ?"

"Listen, just keep quiet till after the final judging, okay?" July purred. "We're supposed to do our demonstrations any minute. We're bound to win, and then we'll share the prize money with you and–"

"Ladies and gentleman," a man's voice interrupted over the loudspeaker. I recognized Mr. Fox, the superintendent of schools. "A photographer and staff writer from *The Daily Sun* are here to photograph and interview our finalists. They'll start in the Household Inventions Division, with the Nice Alarm, represented by club members July Smith, Amy Talbott, Amy Tigard, and Stephen Wyatt!"

Applause. The flash of cameras. Hayley looked like she might cry, Hiccup like he might hic, as a crowd gathered around us, waiting to see the photo shoot.

Smile. Flash. Smile. Flash. The Amys continued to play hostess, gesturing to my invention as if it were a fifty-trillion-dollar jewel. July was a natural, chatting with the judges and Mr. Fox, shaking their hands, tenderly touching the alarm as each shot clicked away.

I felt sick inside, and turned to leave. I caught a glimpse of Ace–what was *he* doing here?–standing behind the crowd, his right brow furrowed.

"Tell them!" Hayley pleaded, pressing my hand.

"You must expose this audacious fraud!" Hiccup insisted.

"What good will it do?" I said. "You heard July. Who'll believe us? Without my invention journals . . ."

"Tony knows!" Hayley said. "We'll find him and–"

"Yes, we'd love to give a demonstration for the cameras!" July announced into a microphone. "Let me coax our fourth club member to help us. He's a little publicity shy." She gripped my arm, tugged me through the bodies of students and parents and teachers, all craning to see.

"Our invention is called the Nice Alarm," she announced in a cool, newscaster-like voice, "because it awakens you *nicely* by tapping you on the shoulder. I'll rest my head here, on the table, pretending I'm asleep on Monday morning. Stephen will set the timer, and we'll see if this alarm can wake me in time for school!"

The crowd laughed. July smiled sweet as her vanilla aroma, laying her head on the cloth-covered table to one side of the alarm. She shot me a glance that meant: *Do it. You don't have a choice. Everyone's watching.* Then she closed her eyes and gave a ladylike snore.

The crowd laughed again.

I moved like a sleepwalker toward the glittering alarm. Beneath the gawdy doodads and mass of cogs and wheels, I found the tiny timer and set it for thirty seconds. I pushed the On button, staring at the twists of wire for a moment, a thought, a worry, poking the back of my brain.

There was something wrong. Something didn't look right. But what?

July stopped snoring. She lay unconcerned, her lips a half-smile, waiting for the sequined glove to awaken her like a prince kissing Sleeping Beauty.

I peered closer at the alarm. Cameras leaned in. A video recorder whirred.

Nothing wrong here, I thought with a mental shake of my head. You're seeing things. The flashy beads and bric-a-brac are distracting you . . .

The crowd began a countdown.

"Ten . . . nine . . ."

Without looking back, without looking forward at

Hayley and Hiccup, I stepped away. Away from the alarm. Away from inventing.

" . . . eight . . . seven . . ."

Then it hit me. In a power surge of memory: that day, last year in sixth grade, when I'd demonstrated my invention for the first time, with Hiccup as my trusting assistant. Things had gone wrong. Painfully wrong. The alarm had whapped instead of tapped, swooping down and karate-chopping Hiccup on the nose.

" . . . six . . . five . . ."

July had made the same mistake. She'd used a pull spring instead of a compression spring, so there was no way to control the speed and weight of the arm. But she didn't know. She couldn't know. She'd copied my alarm without really studying it . . .

. . . and was now seconds away from a possible nose fracture.

It would serve her right.

" . . . four . . . three . . ."

No. It wasn't right to let the Nice Alarm become a laughingstock. To let it become any less than what it could be, what it should be . . .

". . . two . . ."

At the last second, I leaped. Scooped the alarm into my hands. Veered away from July's nose. The arm swung down with a sickening crash, shattering a beaker from the exhibit at the next table.

I heard gasps. A cry. Then July shrieking, "Are you crazy? You ruined my shot! You'd better fix it, Inventor Boy, or else—"

After that, I didn't hear anything. Nothing except the sound of me unbuckling my tool kit, clicking it open, plucking out a hex key, socket head cap screw, and extra compression spring. My fingers worked quickly, expertly, yanking off the sparkles and glitter, unhitching the back cover, the tools clinking the innards, repairing them, restoring them . . .

I was fixing the Nice Alarm. But not for July. Not for the crowd.

I was fixing it for . . . me.

I was done with inventing for other people. Done inventing because other people demanded it of me, expected it of me.

Oh, I still ride, Tony had said the other day, when I asked him why he'd hung up his spurs. *I ride for one reason and one reason only: for the joy of it.*

As I worked, a whoosh of images fountained inside my brain. I could see blueprints for an automatic bed-maker, and shoelaces that didn't break, and a potato chip de-crumbler, maybe even a Diaper Alarm. That oughta come in handy a few months from now . . .

"Steve?"

I glanced up to find Hic and Hayley watching me, bemused expressions on their faces.

"Are you okay?" Hayley asked.

I held up the completed Nice Alarm, cradled in my hands. I turned it this way and that, the gym lights sparking off the tiny cogs and wheels.

I grinned at my friends. Slowly, they grinned back.

"Boy, this is fun," I said.

EPILOGUE

A HIVE OF voices swarmed around me as I left Hobbs gym that day. They buzzed about the Nice Alarm: Tony vouching for my sole ownership of it; July rambling defensively that I hadn't filed for a patent, so it was perfectly all right for her to steal, uh, use the idea; the judges arguing over whether Jefferson Middle School should be disqualified—or if I, only I, should receive first prize—and the entire $2,000 award—for the Nice Alarm.

I walked out the doors with my invention, Hayley and Hiccup at my side, not caring, not listening. After all, I'd already "won" the best prize of the day.

In the parking lot, as we mounted our bikes for home, Ace meandered toward us, a book pack slung over his shoulder. Strange. In all the years I'd known him, I'd never seen him carry a pack. I mean, why should he? He never carried anything except that pencil stub, tucked behind one ear.

"Yo," he said, as if it were the most natural thing in the world for us to run into him on a college campus.

"Hey, Ace." I straddled my bike. "I thought I saw you inside. What are you doing here?"

He shrugged and held out the pack. "Brought these. Just in case."

Bewildered, I took the pack. Unzipped it. Peeked inside.

"What is it?" Hayley asked, craning to see.

I gasped. "My . . . my invention journals! You . . . *you* took them that night?"

He shrugged again. "Thought you might want 'em someday. Besides"–he jerked his head toward the gym–"didn't trust her. Didn't know what she might do."

"*'Her'?*" I asked. "*'She'?*"

He plucked a thread from his shirt. "July," he answered. "My sister."

"Your–sister?" Hiccup said.

It's a legend at my house, July had said about the alarm when I met her for the first time at the Inventor's Club. She'd learned about my inventions and my business name from Ace. She'd probably discovered my journals in his room, maybe even used my original, faulty drawings for the alarm to build the imposter today . . .

And Ace–Mr. John I'm-too-cool-to-care, I'm-too-cool-for-friends Smith–had found her out, and brought the journals, today, *just in case* . . .

"Thanks, man," I said, holding out my hand.

He stared at it for a moment, then arched a brow and clasped my hand in his. We shook, holding on just a bit longer than necessary.

He dropped his hand. Jerked his head at Hiccup, eyeing my friend like I'd seen him do once before, like a cat watching a mouse hole. "Feelin' all right now?" he asked, and a spasm tugged at a corner of his mouth.

"Beyond compare," Hiccup answered.

"Excellent," Ace said. "In spades." He started to saunter away.

In spades . . .

"It was you, wasn't it?" I called after him. "You left the balloon in Hiccup's hospital room. With the playing card—the ace of spades!"

He stopped. Examined a fingernail.

I drew another mental line. "You wrote the column too. In the *Times*. You're Anon E. Mouse. And FH stands for . . . it means . . . For Hiccup."

He turned. Arched one dark brow.

"Oh . . ." Hayley breathed.

"I'm forever honored," Hiccup said, bowing his head.

"You won't . . . ?" Ace began, the rest of the question hanging between us.

I'd never told anyone his real name. I'd certainly never reveal this either.

"Your secret is safe with us," I said.

Hiccup and Hayley nodded.

Ace gave a half wave and ambled off.

***

Mom, Dad, and I went to the Invention Convention® that summer, where I finally met Sterling Patterson, President and CEO of Patterson Enterprises, the man who'd expressed interest in producing the Nice Alarm.

He wasn't as impressed with it as he was with *101 Ways to Bug Your Parents*. He laughed so hard at my book, he sent it to an editor friend at a major publishing house. The editor liked it and laughed too, and published it the following year.

101 Ways to Bug Your Parents was a hit. Such a hit, they asked me to write a sequel. Maybe I'll submit my list of 101 Ways to Bug a Teacher, but only if Hiccup agrees to draw the pictures.

Now the money is rolling in almost as fast as my inventions are rolling out. Once I began inventing for me again, the blocked dam in my brain burst and I've been creating like crazy in the workshop at Patrick Henry High School.

Yeah, that's right. *High school.*

After a long talk with Mom and Dad and Tony, I came up with an optimal solution: I'd spend mornings at Jefferson Middle School, bringing up my grades in history and English, eating lunch with Hayley and Hiccup and Ace. Afternoons I'd spend at Patrick Henry, taking advanced math, science, and engineering classes; and keeping all my inventions there, safe and sound—at least until Dad and I could build a workshop of my own in our garage. After all, I couldn't have my baby sister shoving Chomps-a-Lot (the bubble gum that never loses its flavor) into her ears or teething on the cord of Nuts to You.

And speaking of my baby sister . . .

She was born, healthy and bawling, on December 10.

As soon as the nurses cleaned her up, Mom and Dad let Hayley and me into the delivery room.

"She's amazing!" Hayley said, staring in wonder at the blanketed bundle in Mom's arms. "What are you going to call her?"

"That's up to Steve," Mom said with a tired but warm smile.

234

Dad stroked Mom's hair and added: "We thought since we surprised him with a baby sister, he could surprise us with her name."

"So?" Hayley prompted, a teasing elbow in my ribs. "Have you decided?"

"Yes," I answered, and took a deep breath. "Her first name is Alyssa—"

Hayley gasped.

"—after Hayley's mother."

"That's lovely," Mom murmured and reached out to touch Hayley's hand.

All Hayley managed was "Huh," but she wiped her eyes.

"And her middle name is Marie," I continued, "after Marie Curie, who—"

Mom laughed. "I'm a scientist, Stephen. I *know* who Madame Curie is."

Dad kissed my sister on the top of her peach-fuzzy head. "Welcome to the world, Alyssa Marie."

"She's got the tiniest hands," I marveled, stroking Alyssa's velvety fingerlings.

"She has golfer's hands," Hayley insisted.

"She has her daddy's eyes," Mom said.

"And her mother's nose," said Dad.

Mom chuckled. "Thank goodness it's not the other way around!"

"What does she have of yours, Steve?" Hayley asked.

I searched the tiny face, listened to the mewling voice. "She doesn't look anything like me," I said. "She's just . . . herself."

And as her big brother, I'd do whatever I could to make sure she always stayed that way. To make sure she didn't grow up to do the things expected of her, but only what she expected of herself. To do only what brought her joy.

I peered deeper into her face, checking out her brow, her ears, her chin. Nope. She didn't look a thing like me. We didn't have anything in common at all. Not one single, solitary . . .

Alyssa Marie gazed up at me with unfocused eyes. I put a finger into her hand and she squeezed it. And then . . .

She sneezed.

101 WAYS TO BUG YOUR TEACHER

by Stephen J. Wyatt

PRIVATE AND PERSONAL
NO TRESPASSING
THIS MEANS
YOU!

1. When the teacher says, "Take a seat," answer: "Take it where?"

2. When the teacher calls your name during roll call, yell: "Not here!"

3. When she calls roll, answer: "Yo, mama!"

4. Forget to put your name on your homework.

5. Forget to turn in your homework.

6. Tell the teacher you'll turn in your homework as soon as your parents finish doing it.

7. Tell the teacher you couldn't do your homework because you were too busy watching TV.

8. Fold your homework into a cootie-catcher.

9. Fold your homework into a paper airplane and fly it across the room. Extra points if it crashes on the teacher's desk.

10. Beg your teacher for extensions on reports.

11. Whisper to your neighbor during a test.

12. Argue with your teacher about your test grade.

13. While the teacher is talking, get up to sharpen your pencil. Grind loudly.

14. Drop pencil shavings on the floor.

15. Roll pencils across your desk.

16. Do drum rolls with your pencil. Use the head of the kid in front of you as a cymbal.

17. Never have a pen or pencil so you always have to borrow one from the teacher.

18. Return the teacher's pen or pencil with the end chewed and slobbery.

19. Use crayon for important assignments. Purple crayon.

20. Lean your chair back so that it's balancing on only

two legs. Extra points if you fall over backward.

21. Eat food in class. Loud, crunchy food.

22. Chew gum in class. Extra points if you snap or crack it.

23. When the teacher's back is turned, blow a huge bubble with your gum. Extra points if you pop it.

24. Stick wads of chewed gum on the end of your pencil.

25. Ask if you may be excused to go to the bathroom, even if you just came in from recess or lunch.

26. Ask if you may be excused to go to the bathroom. Then take a tour around your school.

27. When the teacher asks a question, raise your hand. When he calls on you, ask if you may be excused to go to the bathroom.

28. Write so sloppy or small that your teacher can't read your paper.

29. Make rude noises with your mouth or armpit. Blame the noise on the kid sitting next to you.

30. Get a drink while the teacher's talking. Extra points if you gargle.

31. Blurt out the answers to the teacher's questions.

32. When the teacher asks a question, wiggle in your seat, raise your hand, and shout: "I know! I know!"

33. When the teacher asks a question, wave your arm like a palm tree in a hurricane and say: "Pick me! Pick me!" When the teacher calls on you, say: "Never mind."

34. Raise your hand. When the teacher calls on you, look innocent and say: "My hand wasn't up!"

35. Raise your hand again. When the teacher calls on you, say: "I was just stretching!"

36. When the teacher calls on you, ask: "What did you say? I wasn't paying attention."

37. When the teacher calls on you, tell her the longest personal story you know.

38. When the teacher says, "Pay attention, please," ask: "How much should I pay?"

39. When the teacher calls on you, talk so softly that no one can hear you. When asked to speak up, talk more softly than ever.

40. When the teacher calls on you, say: "Finally!"—even if he picked you first.

41. Count how many times your teacher says the word "um." Present your teacher with the grand total at the end of the day.

42. For your book report, choose the shortest book with the most pictures that you can find.

43. Whistle while you work. Extra points if the teacher is talking.

44. Never follow directions.

45. Right after the teacher gives directions, say: "Huh?"

46. Comb, brush, or braid your hair in class.

47. Bring a lizard, mouse, rat, snake, or tarantula to class. "Accidentally" let it go. In the teacher's desk.

48. Work when the teacher is looking at you; don't when he's not.

49. Never let your teacher finish a sentence without an interruption.

50. To everything your teacher says, reply: "That's what YOU think!"

51. Refuse to talk to the substitute teacher "because she's a stranger."

52. Switch seats with your friends so that the substitute's seating chart is all messed up.

53. Allow your cell phone or pager to go off during class.

54. Laugh hard and loud for no reason.

55. Call your teacher by his first name.

56. Call her "Grandma."

57. Call him "Grandma."

58. Throw spit wads.

59. Chew pieces of eraser. Spit them at your neighbor.

60. Read magazines in class.

61. Fall asleep while the teacher is talking. Extra points if you snore.

62. Scratch your fingernails down the chalkboard.

63. Hide all the chalk. The next day, hide the eraser.

64. Pass notes to your neighbor.

65. When the teacher explains something, say: "Well, duh."

66. Every time the teacher explains something, ask: "Is this gonna be on the test?"

67. Never study for tests.

68. Never study. Period.

69. Make up lame excuses for being late.

70. Forget to have your parents write excuses for you being late or sick.

71. Read the first and last chapters of a book, then claim you read the whole thing.

72. Slouch down in your chair and stick your feet up on the desk. Extra points if you take your shoes off. Extra points if you haven't washed your socks recently.

73. Crack your knuckles.

74. When the teacher calls on you, give a wisecrack answer that makes your classmates laugh out loud.

75. Read aloud during silent reading time.

76. Read comic books hidden inside your textbooks.

77. Ask your teacher how old she is. When she answers, stagger backward with your hand on your heart and say: "Wow!"

78. Never put your papers in a binder so they get all crinkly in your backpack.

79. Whenever the teacher asks you to do something, say: "Aw, do we have to?" in a whiney voice.

80. When your teacher leaves the room, quickly erase everything important on the chalkboard.

81. When your teacher leaves the room, yell and scream to disrupt the other classes.

82. Yell "Done!" every time you finish something.

83. Yell "YESSSSSSSSS!" every time you get an answer right.

84. Ask the same question the teacher just finished answering two minutes ago.

85. Daydream instead of listening to instructions, then say: "I don't get it!"

86. Knock a heavy textbook off your desk again and again.

87. Make lots of eraser smudges on your paper so the teacher can't read it.

88. Zip and unzip your backpack or jacket to the beat of your favorite song.

89. Doodle in the pages of your textbook.

90. Doodle on your desk.

91. Tap your feet when the teacher isn't looking; stop when she is looking.

92. When given an assignment, walk up to the teacher and tell him you don't understand it. Before he finishes explaining it, say "I get it," and walk away. Come back a minute later and again ask for help.

93. Never look up words in a dictionary. Always ask your teacher how to spell them.

94. Take out your math book when you're supposed to be studying history.

95. Make animal shadows on the overhead projector screen.

96. Get up and walk between the overhead projector and the screen.

97. While the teacher is talking, roll your eyes, yawn, gaze longingly out the window, then look at the clock every five minutes and sigh. Loudly.

98. Act up in class when your teacher has a guest.

99. Say: "My teacher last year didn't do it this way!"

100. Start gathering your papers and books together ten minutes before class ends.

101. As soon as the bell rings, race out of the room before the teacher excuses you.

MAKING A
CHICKEN MUMMY

MATERIALS NEEDED:

• 1 whole fresh chicken, about 3 pounds. (Do not use a frozen or defrosted chicken.)
• 1 box gallon-size self-sealing freezer bags.
• One large mixing bowl
• One large metal spoon
• 4–6 (one for each week) four-pound boxes of salt (granulated, not rock salt)
• 4–6 (one for each week) one-pound boxes of baking soda
• 1 bottle of olive oil
• 1 box each of cinnamon, nutmeg, and cloves
• Rubber gloves
• Paper towels
• About 2 yards of linen, bandages, or an old sheet, cut into 1" strips

DIRECTIONS:

1. Put on rubber gloves.

2. Remove chicken from wrapper; take out the giblets (neck, gizzard, liver, heart, etc.) and set aside. *

3. Wash the chicken, inside and out, with cool or cold water.

4. Pat chicken completely dry with paper towels. Remember to thoroughly dry the inside of the chicken too.

5. In a large bowl, pour in one box of the salt and one box of the baking soda. Mix well.

6. Coat or dredge the outside of the chicken in the salt and baking soda mixture.

7. Place the chicken inside a freezer bag. Fill the inside cavity of the chicken with the salt and baking soda mixture.

8. Pour the remainder of the salt and baking soda into the bag, making sure it evenly coats all sides of the chicken, especially the wings and drumsticks.

9. Seal the bag. Place the bag inside of a second freezer bag. Set in a cool, dry place for one week.

10. Thoroughly wash the bowl, spoon, rubber gloves, and any surfaces the chicken may have touched, with hot, soapy water. Dry.

11. At the end of the first week, put on the rubber gloves and remove the chicken from the freezer bag. (You will notice a faint, but not unpleasant, poultry odor.)

12. Using paper towels, wipe off the salt into the trash. Pour or wipe out the salt from the inside cavity as well.

13. Repeat with steps 5–9.

14. Each week, until the chicken has dried out (about 4–6 weeks), you will need to remove the chicken from the bag, wipe off the salt, and repeat steps 5–9.

15. When the chicken has completely dried, wipe off the excess salt with damp paper towels. Pat the chicken dry.

16. Rub olive oil into the skin of the chicken.

17. Sprinkle the chicken with ground clove, cinnamon, and nutmeg, and rub into the skin.

18. Wrap the linen or bandage strips around the outside of the chicken until the oil no longer soaks through.

19. Decorate your chicken mummy with "jewels." He is now ready for his funeral procession and entombment!

20. You can have extra fun with this project by: naming your chicken mummy; writing a history of his life, reign, great deeds; building a sarcophagus or tomb for him; creating special treasures for him to take into the afterlife, such as games, books, foods, jewels, etc.

21. You may wish to bury your chicken. Some teachers report they have dug up and unwrapped their chicken mummies more than a year later, and not only did they still look fresh (some with red meat on the bones!), they did not smell!

*Note: You may place the gizzard, neck, liver, etc., into separate glass baby food jars filled with lemon juice, rubbing alcohol, or vinegar, to simulate the canopic jars the Egyptians used to bury the heart and other organs of the great pharaohs.